Keep on inspiring!

They Dance Alone

CHRISTINE LEVEAUX

CAST BUCKET PRESS

This book is available for special discounts for bulk purchases in the United States by colleges and universities, corporations and other organizations. Please contact Cast Bucket Press at castbucketpress@yahoo.com

www.christineleveaux.com

First Printing
Library of Congress Control Number: 2005900159

ISBN 0-9764844-0-4

1.   African American-Fiction. 2. Women-Fiction. I. Title.

Circle Game
Copyright 1966 (renewed) Crazy Crow Music. All rights administered by Sony/ATV Music Publishing, 8 Music Square West, Nashville, TN 37203. All rights reserved. Used by permission.

Book Layout & Design by Rita Mills
Cover Design by Gladys Ramirez
Cover Art by Ted Ellis

The paper used in this publication meets the requirements of the American National Standard for Permanence of Paper for Printed Library Materials Z39.48-1984.

Printed in the United States of America

This book is dedicated to my mother,
Thelma Louise
my grandmother,
Theresa
my great-grandmother,
Virginia
my great-great grandmother,
Grandma Grey
and
my great-great-great grandmother,
name unknown.

ACKNOWLEDGMENTS

I want to first thank God for telling this story through me. Writing this book has been a process of self discovery, revelation and healing and I thank You for the experience.

This book would not have been possible without my mother, Thelma LeVeaux. Thank you for passing along our family history and allowing me to take bits and pieces of the past and create stories based on your recollections. You gave life to this story.

Thanks to my friend Thad Bosley for "discovering the manuscript." If it were not for your positive reaction to the words on a disheveled stack of papers that I asked you to read, those sheets would not have become this book, and would probably still be sitting on a shelf in my closet collecting dust.

Thanks to my sister Noelle, for being my biggest fan and my biggest hero—always a "we thing." Also, I thank my sister Carla, for exampling faith. Thanks to my friend Letitia for raving about my book before reading one word, simply because I wrote it.

I must give credit to two people whom I have

never met, but whom I have believed in throughout this publishing process. Those people are Tom and Marilyn Ross. Thank you for the blueprint, and thank you to Jamellah Ellis for directing me to them.

A wise man once told me everyone needs a team (thanks Ted). I want to recognize my team, Rita Campbell, Tiffany Cowan, and John James. Thank you for allowing me to be the student. Each of you has so much to offer the world; I can't wait to see how you choose to make your mark.

Thank you to Anita Bunkley for your careful reading and thoughtful critique of my manuscript. Your encouraging words fueled me at just the right time.

I must acknowledge Ted Ellis, the artist. Thank you for your enthusiasm and advice, and thank you most of all for so perfectly capturing my vision.

The person most instrumental in the production of the actual book is Rita Mills. You are truly my literary angel! I will never tire of saying thank you.

Thanks especially to my boys, Elijah and Evan, the inspiration for everything I do. You two are the reason that I am able to write so passionately about a mother's love.

They
Dance
Alone

Although this is a work of fiction, many of the names used in this book are family names. This is a gesture of appreciation to those who came before me. My hope and belief is that some part of them will live forever on the pages of this book.

LINEAGE

Mother: Slave woman
Daughter: Elizabeth

Mother: Elizabeth
Daughter: Rose

Mother: Rose
Daughter: Virginia

Mother: Virginia
Daughter: Pauline

Mother: Pauline
Daughter: Eva

Mother: Eva
Daughter: Dorothy

Mother: Dorothy
Daughter: Terry

SLAVERY

1

SLAVERY

Terry stared intently at the two women standing in front of her. One woman was round and short with light brown skin and natural hair mixed black and gray; the other woman was taller and leaner with brown skin and big brown eyes. The women were different, but both beautiful. Terry continued to study the women, one whose name she shared, the other whose face she shared. Eva Theresa, or Terry, as most people called her, was the daughter of Dorothy Mitchell, and the granddaughter of Eva Reynolds. All of her life these two women painstakingly shaped and molded Terry into the woman she had become.

As Terry prepared for her wedding, and even thought about having children of her own one day, she hoped that she could be the wife and mother that these women had been. She thought about how her mother and grandmother sacrificed for their family. She thought about the hard times that both women had endured, knowing that she had been shielded from most of them. What made them so strong? Terry wished she could look deep into these women, through them, to their past, and back even further to those who came before them. She believed that understanding who they were and where they came from would give her insight into herself as a woman, wife and someday as a mother. But Terry would never know that the strength she so admired in her mother and her grandmother also lived deep inside of her, passed down through her ancestors.

My mother came to see me every night until I was around twelve years old.

This was extraordinary as most mothers were separated from their children by great distances and after a year or so would become weary of threatening their lives to sit with their children for an hour or two. But my mother was persistent, and almost every night for as long as I can remember, she would steal away onto Master Thompson's land and lay with me, and tell me about my father and my brothers. She told me that my father was born a free man, and because of this, I should always consider myself free. My father had lived in Illinois as a child and had been smuggled with his two brothers down the misery river into slavery. This same river took my two brothers down to the deep South where the slaveholders were known for their extreme belief in Christianity and their extreme cruelty.

I found out years after slavery ended that the real name of the misery river was the Missouri River. I thought it was amazing that the name of this river sounded so much like what the river embodied for so many. The misery river separated husbands from their wives, ripped babies from their mothers' breasts, and kidnapped and enslaved free men, women and children.

My mother also told me of life in Africa before *they* came. Of course, stories about Africa were figments of my mother's imagination. We were so far removed from those years that she could only relate stories that had been passed down through generations. But the stories she told were of honor and family, commitment and excellence. Night after night, she spoke of slaves that tried to escape, and of those that did actually reach freedom. Oh, the stories she would tell of the life they lived in New York City, living right next to white folks, shopping with them and eating with them and working side by side with them, for wages, just like the white folks. Night after night she would tell me that we deserved more than the life we lived as slaves. She told me that I wouldn't be a slave forever. She would see to that. She talked about her plans to make me free . . . soon.

My mother devised a plan for both of us to escape when I was around seven years old. My mother was a personal servant to Master Brennan's oldest daughter Lucy. Master Brennan had acquired slaves through his marriage to Master Thompson's sister Ms. Anne. The South was divided into two types of white folks; those who owned slaves and those who did not. Master Brennan came from a family who had never owned slaves. The reason why was unclear. Master Brennan did not come from a poor family, or from a family philosophically opposed to slavery. His father was an educated man, an accountant, and therefore did not depend on the land directly for his family's survival. This usually did not stop a white man from having one or two servants, but in Master Brennan's family slave labor was considered unnecessary.

Slave masters who had not been accustomed to owning slaves took on two forms. An inexperienced slave master might attempt to masque his ignorance

with brutality. These were the most dreaded of masters. Intoxicated with their newly acquired power; there
were no limits to the transgressions they perpetrated
against the slaves. Having always looked in from the
outside, they did not understand that boundaries existed, even in the master's handling and treatment of
slaves. The inexperienced slave master might take on a
different form, showing relative kindness and consid-
eration to the enslaved population. Not having been
conditioned to hate, degrade, mistreat, violate, and de-
humanize slaves, they felt uncomfortable in their new
role as the *southern slave master*, and shied away from
beating and punishing their slaves.

Master Brennan resembled the latter of the two
slave owners. Master Brennan ran his plantation as a
business. The slaves were given tasks, and were ordered
to complete them in the time and in the manner that
Master Brennan expected. His slaves worked eighteen
to twenty hour days just as other slaves, but they were
fed adequately and did not live in constant fear that
their day would end with a lashing, or that they would
be locked away in darkness for days, or that an overseer
might knock them unconscious in the field without
explanation. Acknowledging his inexperience and in-
difference to the institution of slavery, he left the management, trade and punishment of the slaves to Master
Thompson. This suited Master Thompson just fine,

who, as the only male heir of his father's estate, considered all of the slaves his.

Master Brennan's daughter, Miss Lucy, was engaged to be married to a man who lived in Ohio. My mother accompanied Miss Lucy on several trips to this free state and as they traveled through woods and mountains, and alongside swamps and rivers, my mother took note of all that she saw. My mother told me that slaves were treated differently when they entered a free state. Recognizing that slavery was not widely accepted in these states, masters and mistresses alike tempered their behavior so as not to appear uncivilized. Because of this, there were many opportunities to escape, and there seemed to be many people who were sympathetic to the plight of the slave.

The temptation to flee was great, and yet my mother never seriously considered her escape because she claimed that life as a freedwoman would be meaningless if her daughter remained in slavery. Instead, she used each trip to plot our departure from the South.

Late into the night on the eve of our intended escape, there was a loud commotion in the center of the slave quarters. As we looked through cracks in the wood walls, straining to see what the excitement was, a slave knocked on the door and told us that Master Thompson wanted all slaves to come to the watering hole. By the time we reached the watering hole a large group of slaves had already gathered. They formed a circle around what I could see was several white men on horses with torches. I could not see what most of the slaves were looking at, which seemed to be down on the ground. But once I pushed my way through I saw him; a young slave man named Johnny who had run away almost a year earlier.

Because Johnny had been gone so long without any word of his whereabouts, we were all convinced that he had made it to freedom. And he had. Johnny had lived and worked as a free man in New York, but Johnny did not realize that the slave catchers were feverishly pursuing him. One evening on his way home from the stockyard where he worked, Johnny was captured by three slave catchers who had been tipped off by an Irish worker whom Johnny had argued with the week before. Johnny was quickly transported back to the South, to an uncertain fate.

Now, Johnny laid naked on his back with his arms and legs spread apart. His hands and feet were tied to iron stakes driven into the ground. He had been severely beaten. Blood gushed from the right side of his head and his left eye was swollen shut.

Master Thompson was also in the middle of the circle. He was enraged, screaming and striking Johnny with the butt of a pistol. We stood around him, filled with dread in our hearts for our brother in bondage.

Master Thompson exclaimed that he would teach Johnny and the rest of us a lesson so that we would never think about running away again. But more ominously, he proclaimed that Johnny would never be able to run from him again.

As Johnny pleaded for his life, Master Thompson quickly spun the pistol around and pulled the trigger, firing off a shot. We all scattered, fearing for our lives, not knowing how the lesson would be taught. Master Thompson barked at us to return immediately. We reluctantly returned to find Johnny incoherently begging for Master's mercy, his life spared for the moment. To our relief Master Thompson put his pistol away and we felt assured that Johnny would not lose his life that night at the watering hole. But mixed with relief was confusion and anticipation. Why had Master Thompson shackled Johnny to the ground in this way? Before the question could fully form in our minds, Master Thompson grabbed a torch from one of the men and lit fire to Johnny's feet. We looked on in horror and amazement at Master's cruelty. With his hands and feet fettered, Johnny was helpless against the fire that threatened to engulf his entire body. Some of us tried to kick dirt onto Johnny's feet, but Master Thompson charged at us with the torch, terrorizing the group.

Johnny screamed as he continued to burn, no words now, only shrieks of pain. Slaves became accustomed to many horrific sounds, the piercing crackle of a whip making contact with skin, the desperate and futile pleading of a slave attempting to avoid his punishment, the shrilling sob of a heartbroken mother whose child has been torn from her arms on the trading block. But none of these were as deafening as the screams of a man who helplessly watches his flesh burn away from his bones, who feels his muscles disintegrate from the heat of the flames, who smells the sulfur escaping into the night air, the by-product of his burning flesh. Each second that Johnny burned felt like hours, but after several minutes of this torture, Master Thompson ordered two slaves to douse the flames with buckets of water waiting nearby.

I laid awake all that night unable to shake the sight of the charred remains of Johnny's feet. When the time came for me to begin my journey to freedom, both my body and my mind were paralyzed. My limbs felt too heavy to lift off the ground, and my head was too full of images from that night of horror to contemplate my escape. And so morning came and I laid perfectly still, having buried any thoughts of running away, ever.

When Master Thompson received the news that my mother had escaped, he and Master Brennan interrogated me for days about my mother's plans. My entire being resisted the two men. My determination to protect my mother was so great that when I spoke, my voice was strong and steady. When I raised my hand to shield myself from Master Thompson's unrelenting blows, my hands did not tremble and shake as I had expected. In the past, less intense confrontations had caused my heart to beat so fiercely that I believed it would leap from my chest, and my breath became so short that I thought I would surely stop breathing. My mother had given me life, and in this instance, with her life in my hands, I was unmoved. I would protect her life with my own.

Throughout the assault, I continually assured them that I knew nothing of her plans to run away. Master Thompson was infuriated, and although slave children my age were not whipped with cow skin, Master Thompson struck my face with the back of his hand with enough force to knock out two of my teeth. He also ordered me to work in the cotton fields along side the older slaves.

For each of the sixty-four days that my mother was free, I welcomed the burden laid upon me by Master. My mother's freedom was in every pod of cotton that I pulled from its stem, and in every blister that festered on my virgin hands, and in every fainting spell I succumbed to. I rejoiced in every aspect of my toil, because it represented freedom for my mother. I spent hours in the field, day dreaming about my mother as a free woman. She wore a beautiful pink dress, like the one Mistress Sarah, Master's wife wore. She worked as a laundress, or a seamstress, or a cook, or she cleaned houses. These were all jobs that she said former slave women were suited for. My mother had her own money, and she would go to the market and choose from an array of the ripest fruits and vegetables. She would prepare a feast for herself and the other people in the boarding house, who had become her family. Most of all, my mother was safe, and she was happy.

As the days passed I heard varying accounts of my mother's fate. She was alive. She was dead. She was free. Working in the field, side by side with the older slaves, I would overhear bits and pieces of coded conversation about my mother's whereabouts and condition.

Early on, they received word from an elderly aunt who had cared for my mother when she was younger. This woman, now old and crippled, no longer served a purpose for her slave master and was sold to a family who supplied safe cover for runaway slaves as they navigated through the swamps and forests of the southern terrain. The woman claimed that she had seen my mother, cared for her, and fed her before my mother was carried away, concealed on the bottom of a wagon with one other runaway. This news lifted our spirits, and for several days there was a sense of excitement. Though we remained enslaved we felt triumphant, free in our spirit because one of our own had reclaimed control of her body and mind.

My mother was free. On the night that I chose bondage over freedom, I came to understand that for my mother, survival depended on her being free. And so I knew that this was the only possible outcome for her. Although life was empty and the nights long, thoughts of my mother reaching freedom sustained me. Because of this I was unprepared for the possibility of a different outcome. When I heard the news that a slave woman's body had been found in a swamp several miles north of us, the sea of green and white cotton plants turned black, and even the southern heat could not keep my face from turning ice cold. My consciousness was regained with the help of the overseer's foot thrusting into my ribs. Ordered back to work, I listened intently to the details of the story.

Slaves who ran knew that the risks were infinite. Slaves might elude man, but they also had to survive the elements, being careful not to eat the fruits of a poisonous plant, or fall prey to the wild boar, serpent, or crocodile. Their steps had to be chosen with care, avoiding areas with sinking earth and deep holes camouflaged with vines and leaves. The woman was the apparent victim of a water moccasin. Hoping that the water would hide her scent from the bloodhounds; she met with an enemy more formidable than the white man. Now her body would be drug around from plantation to plantation as a reminder to all slaves of the perils of life outside of the plantation.

As the slaves communicated through words, sounds, whistles and song, it became clear that this unfortunate woman was not my mother. Having some knowledge of the trail used by those assisting my mother, an elderly uncle assured us that she would not have been in the area where the woman's body was found. I had no choice but to believe him. His words gave me the strength to wake up each morning and complete my tasks without collapsing into tears, overcome by the doubt that each new day brought. I would wait to receive confirmation of what I already knew in my heart, my mother was alive.

After several days, an older slave woman who we called Aunt Nel, approached me with a message that had been sent from my mother. She told me that my mother had reached free land; she had made it safely to Ohio, and then to New York. Now, hope filled the vacuum created by her absence, and I was once again contented to work harder and longer than anyone else in the field. I welcomed each morning as another day that my mother was free. But this hope was soon dashed by word that my mother had been captured and was in route back to the South.

My mother never spoke of her escape, or of

her days as a free woman. I thought it must have been too painful to discuss, having tasted the sweet nectar that was freedom only to be thrust back into the bitter life that slavery promised. I thought my mother might have been better off had she never experienced life outside the oppressive southern slave system. After she returned, she was more defiant and obstinate than ever. This, coupled with Master Thompson's vigilance in punishing those who attempted to escape, and especially those who succeeded in their effort, ensured my mother a life filled with too much work, too little food, and far too many lashings. When my mother was finally able to slip away in the night to see me, she held me and rocked me and kissed me. I tried to tell her why I did not follow her instruction, how sorry I was that she was now, once again, enslaved, but she stopped me, and assured me that she was right where she wanted and needed to be, close to me.

For me, work in the fields continued after my mother returned to the plantation, and it was there that I heard what my mother was unwilling to tell me. She had not been captured; rather she had turned herself over to the authorities. Once she received word that I had remained on Master Thompson's plantation, she made plans to return.

Although slavery was a southern establishment, the North was a full, willing and cooperative partner.

Runaway slaves were not just fugitives in the South, but also in the North, making it illegal to assist or harbor a runaway slave in any way, anywhere in this country. This obligated the white man, woman or child to disclose any information they had about a possible runaway slave. Knowing this, my mother presented herself to a family having lunch in a field and identified herself as a runaway slave. The man, fixated on the possible reward associated with her capture, left his family and turned my mother in to the authorities.

She gave up her freedom for me, and then she selflessly shielded me from the reality of her capture, recognizing that the burden was too much for my heart to bear. She never offered any details, and I never asked, but I knew the truth; I knew that I was covered by a love that caused one person to give up her hopes, her dreams, and possibly her life for me.

I only saw my mother outside of the sleeping quarters once a year during the Christmas Holiday. The slaves from the Brennan and Thompson plantations were allowed to come together for one day during the holiday. Those were always festive times. There was plenty to eat, and for the adults, plenty of spirits to drink. There was music and there was laughter and there was dancing. It was during these celebrations that I saw my mother at her most joyful and her most sorrowful.

Around dusk, the jubilance would fade, the

laughter would cease, and the smiles would disappear. The mood of the slaves would change, and the dance of the widowed slave women would begin. Slave women were considered widowed if their husband had been killed by the cruel hands of a murderous master, or if they had been shipped South down the misery river, or if they had escaped and found freedom in the North or in Canada. The dance began with the eldest widow. While the others locked arms around her, signaling a collective strength, the elder began to rock from side to side, embracing herself, as if she were embracing her husband. The women patiently waited their turn and one by one they entered the center of the circle, and they danced alone. Each woman began her dance the same way, with her arms wrapped tightly around her body. Many women danced violently around the circle, moaning and weeping for their loved ones. Some crumbled to the ground, overcome by their pain and anguish. Some women sang while they danced and they prayed. They prayed that their husbands were alive and in good health. They prayed that their husbands had not met with the misfortune of having a merciless master, and mostly they prayed that their husbands had safely reached freedom, and that they were no longer in bondage.

My mother's dance began as the others, with her

arms around herself. Her movements were slow. Her voice was soft. I watched her intently as the tears began to fall. Her love for my father was great. They had had plans and dreams. Because my father was once free they had envisioned a life together with their children away from the brutality and inhumanity of the South. My father loved my mother enough to die for her. And he did. To the very end he defended and protected my mother. This fact tormented her as she lived on this earth without him. As she danced she cried out to the heavens, proclaiming that she would join him soon, so that husband and wife could again be one.

The children sat right outside the circle, watching their mothers pay homage to their fathers. Tears streamed down the children's faces, many of whom like me, never met their fathers, but we felt the agony of our mothers, and we cried their tears. As the men looked on, they too grieved because those being honored were their brothers, and uncles, and fathers, and sons. And each man grieved for himself and for his family, knowing that next holiday his wife might patiently wait her turn to enter the center of the circle.

The last trip my mother ever made to see me, she was quite ill. She had a very high fever. She was fatigued and suffering from dementia. Instead of talking, she slept, and I cared for her, rubbing her body down with wet rags, trying to break the fever that had taken over her body. As my mother slept, I looked at her in a way I had never looked at her before. She always symbolized such strength, but now she looked so fragile. Her five-foot frame looked worn. As I studied her face I noticed the wrinkles, reflecting the worry that made her old beyond her years. My mother's hands were beautiful, her palms and fingers were rough and calloused, but the back-side of my mother's hands revealed a maze of large shapely veins. As I stared at the veins, I tried to imagine as far back as possible the women who also shared those veins. The veins told a story of power, perseverance and determination. Then, I looked at my own hands, just like hers. The veins in my hands represented life; their thickness represented the strength passed down from my mother to me. I had her hands, and her strength.

I cared for her all night, until the last minute when I knew she needed to go so that she would not be discovered. We tried to get her up, but she could not move, and it was now too late for Paul Homer or Elliot, two of my mother's uncles, to carry her all the way back to the Brennan plantation. We devised a plan to sneak her out in the morning. She was better then, the fever had broken, but we were surprised that morning by an early visit from Master Thompson.

We later found out that someone had told a slave who lived in the Master's house that a slave woman from the Brennan plantation was coming around at night to have relations with one of Thompson's slaves.

When Master Thompson found my mother in the quarters, he dragged her out to the hook. As we pleaded, he hoisted her fragile body up to the hook and he beat my mother like I had never seen him beat anyone before. But she was so frail. Surely he recognized that she could not take the lashings that a man could take, but his anger was uncontrollable. He would beat her and then rest, demanding that I bring him lemonade, only me. He wanted me to be there to witness the punishment given to my mother for making me believe my life mattered. He continued in this way for half of the day. He beat her until he was exhausted, angered at having discovered that this woman had sneaked onto his property night after night, believing that she had the right to form a bond with her daughter. How dare she teach one of his slaves that she was worthy of love, and not just any love, but a mother's love?

My mother hung on that hook for a full day after Master finished beating her. The sun blazed down on her tattered back as it burned the gashes shut. My mother hung there and died, and then she hung for two more days, because Master would not let any of the slaves remove my mother from the hook. I wept, I wept, and I wept and I wept. Slave life was designed so that a slave would not feel, and perhaps this was good, so when they ripped away children, husbands, or loved ones, slaves would feel very little loss, because the bond had never been formed. That person was never claimed by another, never nurtured, protected, or loved. But I did claim my mother; I loved my mother so dearly and now I felt the loss that so few slaves could experience. My mother was security in a life of uncertainty and cruelty and degradation. Now my security was gone, and I did not know if I could live in this life without her.

The night they removed my mother's body from the hook, they took me from the slave quarters. Word was I was going to live in the Master's house. I had heard about life in the Big House. I might wait on the mistress, or one of Master's four daughters. I would bathe them, and brush their hair, and eat their leftovers, and sleep on a pallet rather than the hardened earth, and enjoy the warmth of the fire that burns throughout the night. Master must have felt some remorse. Somewhere in his soul he was sorry for killing a mother in front of her child. He wanted to make up for it, not to me, but to God. Master was a religious man and I was sure this was an attempt to repent; this was an attempt at forgiveness.

As the wagon approached the Big House, my spirits lifted. Somehow this was the beginning of the freedom that my mother so desired for me. I knew it. But instead of stopping at the Big House, the wagon passed it and stopped in front of a small wood shack far behind the Big House in the woods. They put me in this little house, and this was where I stayed for three days. There was only room for a bed, but because I had never slept on a bed, this was a small luxury as I awaited my fate.

When Master opened the door on the fourth night, I was happy to see him, certain that he had come to apologize and to repent to God in my presence. But instead, he pushed me back flat against the bed and pressed all of his weight on top of me. I could barely breathe. I thought, *He has brought me here to kill me. I will surely suffocate under his weight.* But then he lifted himself up on his knees and fumbled with his pants. I did not know what he was looking for, but he must have found it because the fumbling stopped and then he pressed all of his weight back on me harder than before, and I thought my chest would collapse, but that sensation was soon replaced by a sharp pain between my legs. Master was thrusting deeply into me, hard and fast, and with each thrust I felt my insides tearing apart. Oh the pain. I tried to cry out, but Master's hand covered my mouth and most of my face, making it difficult for me to breathe. The thrusts became more and more powerful, and the pain was deeper, as tears streamed down my face. I wished for a different fate, my mother's fate. *Please*

Masuh, whup me. I can bear that pain, but this, this pain I cannot bear. The pain is between my legs, and in each of my finger tips. The pain is in my eyes, and in my head, the pain is in my heart and in my veins. With one last thrust, Master Thompson fell on to my body, and I hoped and prayed that his weight would kill me to stop the pain.

It was then that I learned never to expect mercy from a white man. It was then that I learned to plead for mercy only from a force more powerful than the white man, a force that I could not see or touch, but a force that I had to believe existed. My very survival depended on this. Once I had experienced the hopelessness and despair of slavery, as a woman, I truly understood the slaves' steadfast dependence on God.

My mother's faith in God had baffled me when I was young. I could not understand how she could praise a force that was all-powerful and all-knowing, yet allowed slaves to suffer the way we did. How could she lift up the God who had allowed her husband to be killed, and her children to be shipped off, far away to the deep South to live a wretched existence, even by slave standards? How could she exalt this God who allowed her to experience hunger, and torture, and rape, and loss? I did not understand my mother's devotion to this unworthy God.

I thought that slaves were weak for waiting on

God to deliver them to safety rather than taking up the cause themselves. I believed that our reliance on God kept us in bondage. Our belief in God kept us obedient, and fearful, and meek. Because we knew that the "meek shall inherit the earth," and we knew that "those that suffer will see God," and we knew that "many are the afflictions of the righteous, but the Lord delivers him out of them all," and we knew that "they that sow in tears shall reap in joy." And so the masses of us were content to wait on this unworthy God to deliver us to the Promised Land.

I became a Christian in that dark shed far behind Master Thompson's house in the woods. I owed my survival during those years in that dark shed to God...He was my beacon of light. He was hope. Some days I would pray to God from sunrise to sunset that Master Thompson would not come to visit that night. And when Master Thompson did not come, I praised God all night long, believing that He had heard my prayers, and answered them ...that night. My deep belief in God gave me a will to live and a will to fight for survival. Now, I recited with conviction words that I repeatedly had heard my mother speak: "Though I walk in the midst of trouble, thou will revive me, thou shall stretch forth thine hand against the wrath of mine enemies, and thy right hand shall save me."

Many years after the darkness, I learned that my

mother did share my fate. My mother spent time in the same shack, on the same bed, with Master thrusting into her petite frame as he did mine. She was sent away when she became pregnant with me by a slave man named Henry, who was killed when Master found out that he was my father. Henry was also my mother's husband, and the father of her two male children that were sold from her on the slave trading block.

When Master Thompson purchased my mother, she and my two brothers were displayed as a family. But on the trading block, the man was considered a stud, with no emotional ties to his brood mare or offspring. Therefore, he was not considered part of the unit. Foreshadowing Master's depravity, he chose not to buy the two children; instead a slave owner from the deep South bought my brothers and carried them far away from my mother. Henry was also sold earlier that day. As he was taken away he strained to look into his wife's eyes, to memorize her face, knowing that this was the last time he would see her. But several years later, he was acquired by Master Thompson, who had unknowingly reunited husband and wife.

Master shot Henry in the head. Even with the cruelty that slaveholders showed slaves, this was unheard of. Most importantly, because each slave translated into profit, and to kill a healthy strong slave man, was to kill a portion of your profits. Also, as a Christian, which

Master Thompson was this lack of restraint and emotional retaliation went against the teachings of the Bible. I also learned that I was sent back to Master Thompson's shortly after my birth as further punishment to my mother.

From the very moment that a slave woman gave birth to her child, she began preparing for the day when that child would be taken from her. My mother's day came just four weeks after I was born. Master Thompson personally came and tore me from my mother's arms. Her body was still swelled from pregnancy; her breasts were still engorged with milk to nourish her newborn baby. Her heart was still filled with the love that only a mother feels when she first looks into the eyes of the life that she has sustained within her for nine months. On that day, when my mother's pain was almost too much to bear, Master Thompson took her only joy away.

Before he left, he bent down to my mother, who was on her hands and knees pleading with him to leave me with her just a little longer, and whispered in her ear, promising her that I, too, would be violated by him night after night.

She knew that I would feel the pain and despair that she felt. She knew that there was little she could do to prevent this from happening, and so she did what she could. She talked to me, held me, and showed me love. She planted the seed that told me I was worthy of more. She planted in me the will to live, the will to survive, and so each night, for two years, Master Thompson violated my body, but he did not violate my soul.

My daughter was born in 1866. For a long time there were whisperings that there was no more slavery, that slaves had been released, that slaves were free. But Master Thompson and the slave holders around us had not received the news because life went on much like it had always. My daughter, Rose, was conceived after slavery had been abolished. When freedom actually reached our plantation, there were many reunions between lovers, husbands and wives, children and parents, but none for my daughter. Born the child of a slaveholder, there was no father who longed to see her. My mother was dead, my father was dead, and my brothers had been sent away long before I was born. We had no one. She had no one . . . but me.

Freedom meant a lot of things to slaves, the very least of which was *freedom*. Many of us women found ourselves alone, having never had a husband. And so, life after slavery was difficult for the freedwoman. Unable to survive on my own, I chose the life of a slave again. I became a servant for the Coleman family; my compensation was room and board for my daughter and myself. This provided the shelter and security that we needed. Many men and women around me were dying. There was talk that the whole of the race was diseased or starving, and so I chose the life I knew: a life that meant survival for me and survival for my daughter.

LYNCHING

2

LYNCHING

My mother taught me how to knead dough with my fists, the palm of my hands, and the tips of my fingers.

Once I was old enough, she passed along her secrets to me, saying, "Virginia, the key to a perfect pie is the crust. It must be free of lumps, buttery, and once cooked, it *must* be flaky." I cherished these times with my mother; cooking, learning, talking, and most of all tasting the sweet apple, cherry, peach, rhubarb, and boysenberry mixtures that filled the uncooked pie crust.

Where we lived, my mother was known for two

things; her angelic voice and her heavenly pies. No baptism, wedding or funeral was complete without one of Rose Johnson's pies, and so my mother saw to it that each family had a pie to enjoy, no matter whether the occasion was to mourn the loss of a life, or to celebrate the start of a new one.

My mother began singing when she was a young girl. After the war she and my grandmother Elizabeth, went to live with the Coleman family. My mother did not talk much about her childhood, but when I helped her prepare food, it often reminded her of her life at the Coleman's and she would tell her story. She said:

> "Each night before we went to bed, my mother would brush my hair, 50 strokes just as she did for Miss Jane, Miss Sarah, and Miss Ruth. She attended to their needs all day. From our room, I could constantly hear the girls calling, "Elizabeth, Elizabeth." My mother would bathe them, and dress them, and brush their hair. She would fix their breakfast, wash their sheets, and clean their rooms. She would prepare their lunch, mend their dresses, and make sure they practiced their lessons. She kept watch over them as they played near the magnolia tree, kissed their bumps and cleaned their cuts. She baked delicious treats for them, cooked dinner, bathed them brushed their hair, and sang

to them. She held them tight and kissed them goodnight, then cleaned the pots, and mopped the floor, and made preparations for dinner the following night. By the time she came to our room it was near 11:00 o'clock at night. But, instead of falling into the bed from exhaustion, she would brush my hair, while I recited the day's lesson for her.

For most of the day I was not to be seen. Mr. and Mrs. Coleman allowed me to stay at the house with my mother, and they felt that since they gave us a place to stay, they had appropriately compensated her, so she made no money for all of the work she did. I did not understand why or how my mother could work so hard, and not be paid any wages for it. My mother explained to me that this was the life that she had to live, but it would not be the life that I would live.

My mother arranged for me to clean the parlor each day while the children had their lesson in the next room. I was able to hear everything that the children recited. When their lesson was done, and they went to play near the magnolia tree, my duty was to clean that room as well. I would collect the discarded lessons from the previous day. After cleaning, I was sent back to my room where I ate dinner, usually a much smaller portion of what the children ate, but without any meat, and then I quietly practiced my lessons. No one bothered me. No one ever came to the room to talk to me or check on me, so I was left to study my lessons for hours, and I did."

This was the story my mother told of her life with my grandmother Elizabeth and the Colemans. My mother was a diligent student, learning not only from books, but also learning social behavior, proper hygiene, and most of all music from the Colemans. As she grew older, she too began to cook, clean and assist the Coleman children with their daily routine. Each afternoon when the children practiced the piano, my mother's task was to turn the music filled pages. My mother studied the musical notes and the children's hand movements, often singing the melody under her breath.

One such afternoon, when my mother was about ten years old, Miss Sara played a song that moved my mother in such a way that her usually murmured singing became strong and as she belted out the words to Amazing Grace. All those in earshot stopped what they were doing and came to see who had produced such a splendid sound. She said that even her mother, who worked without interruption, paused to investigate this unfamiliar sound that now filled the home. The Colemans were so impressed with my mother's singing that they began to use her to entertain their guests.

Her voice was the reason my mother and father first met. As my mother prepared for her performance at the Colemans yearly Christmas party, a young man named Bobby Johnson was in the next room helping his father put the finishing touches on a breakfront that they had made for the Colemans. My father said that my mother's singing rendered him powerless. Unable to concentrate on his work, he quietly moved toward the music hoping to glimpse perfection. When he peered into the room, he saw a petite Negro woman. He thought surely she could not possess this voice, soft and sweet, yet powerful and commanding. But as he watched he realized that the melody left her lips, then bounced throughout each room in the house. It seemed to rise to the ceiling, then fall back down to the floor. Her voice filled the house, soothing and comforting all those within. My father felt privileged to be in the Coleman home at that moment, and as he marveled at her talent, he realized that the woman who was singing was as beautiful as the music itself, as beautiful as he often remarked afterwards, as the flower she had been named after.

Beautiful. My mother had never been called beautiful, never thought of herself as beautiful. My mother had always been embarrassed and ashamed of how she looked. Her fair skin and freckled face were a manifestation of the violation of her mother's body, her long sandy hair, evidence of a crime committed. She was not born of love, but was the result of hate, brutality and domination. Teased by the other Negro youth, she felt cursed—a bastard child, unaccepted even by those of whom she was a part. But now she was beautiful in the eyes of Bobby Johnson, the son of Tommy Johnson, one of the wealthiest and most respected Negroes in town.

My grandfather, Poppy Tommy, was a skilled wood carver and carpenter. He was as skilled in the art of wood carving as men in his ancestry who had been plucked from the West African soil. This was his family's gift, inherited, not learned. As a slave, his work had been so extraordinary that his owner began selling my grandfather's service to people throughout the area. His owner realized great gains due to my grandfather's workmanship. My grandfather realized none, but because his value was so great, his master set my grandfather apart from the other slaves and allowed his family to live together in a structure just slightly more sturdy than a shack. This one act enabled my grandfather to experience an emotion that few slave men would ever experience. The flimsy structure was his home. He was permitted to live in it with his wife and sons. He was the head of his home and the center of his family.

He was *proud* . . . few slave men had any understanding of this concept. Working someone else's land, living on someone else's property, often unable to claim his wife and children as his own, unsure of where he may lay his head from one night to the next. The male slave was stripped of his manhood. But for my grandfather, his manhood was restored through a one room wooden structure distinguishing the people inside of it as his own.

Although he was still the property of Master Jones, my grandfather took ownership of his family by protecting them and caring for them. As a protection, he did not teach his two older sons the art of carpentry. Often seeing Master Jones collect money for my grandfather's services, he felt used and exploited. His small taste of independence made him hungry for more, and at times he felt that he had been cursed to experience a hint of freedom. He did not want his sons to feel the frustration, or the unrelenting despair, of knowing how it felt to love a child, and a wife, living each day as their protector, but knowing how fragile this protection was and how vulnerable and powerless he was to the whims of an unpredictable slave master. No, he would rather they work the fields with the other slaves, and never ingest the taste of freedom.

When freedom did come, my grandfather was mentally prepared to become the head of his home, but many former slaves were disillusioned by their liberation. One day enslaved, the next free; one day property, the next a *man* with free will and responsibility for his own life, and the life of his wife and children.

My grandfather told us about life after the war. He explained that the soldiers left and life was not much different than before, but eventually the soldiers returned and brought with them a new life for the freed slaves. Negroes controlled the government, went to school, and worked for wages. The South, so badly damaged from the war, began the process of rebuilding. My grandfather's services were greatly needed and he continued his work as a wood carver and carpenter, but now it was he who was compensated. As the war torn South was rebuilt both physically and figuratively, my grandfather took his position as one of the elite within the community of newly freed men.

Each Christmas, my mother made three pies. My aunts also prepared dishes to bring to my grandfather's house up on the hill. All of the children liked to go to Poppy Tommy's. His house sat on a high hill surrounded by hundreds of tall pine trees. His house was white with a long porch across the front of it. Poppy Tommy wanted his house to look just like some of them white folks' houses that he helped to build.

Three of his sons, including my father, lived in houses on the road leading up to the hill. The fourth and youngest son, my Uncle Joe, did not have a family of his own and still lived with my grandfather and grandmother. At Poppy Tommy's house we could get lost in the trees, or play horse shoes in the grass, or cool off in the stream that ran on the other side of the hill. Most of all, we could talk and play with our Uncle Joe. All of the children loved Uncle Joe. He was always making us laugh, and always giving us candy. We wanted to be at Poppy Tommy's because this was where we felt safe, loved, and protected.

Before eating Christmas dinner, my father and his brothers each spoke and prayed on behalf of his family. Then my grandfather would say a prayer for his entire family praising God and asking God to bless us as He had the past year.

Each family gathering would end with Poppy Tommy talking about how white folks didn't know how to do anything when Negroes were slaves and they still didn't, so they needed us. He got this from a man he once traveled several days to hear speak. Negroes, the man had said, and my grandfather believed, should keep on doing what they did as slaves, but now for pay. My grandfather believed if we left white folks alone, they would leave us alone, and so he worked hard to provide for his family and didn't cause any trouble. He was always respectful and helpful, and so the whites, most of whom he had worked for at some point, liked having him around.

After slavery ended, Poppy Tommy taught his trade to his two younger sons. At first Poppy Tommy accompanied them and oversaw each job, but soon he stayed back and let them do most of the work. Before sending them on their own, my grandfather explained the perils of their job, the dangers of entering a white man's home, and more importantly, a white woman's home day after day. I remember hearing Poppy Tommy warn my father and Uncle Joe that the greatest misfortune for a Negro man was to become the object of desire, admiration, lust or obsession for a white woman. They were instructed to always keep their heads down, and not to make eye contact or conversation. They went to every job together, no matter how small, and they were never to be out of each other's sight for long. This suited them just fine. The only time they argued was when my father felt that Uncle Joe had been too friendly to one of the women in whose home they worked. They were very close as brothers. They worked all day with each other, then after work Uncle Joe usually stayed for dinner or we all might go up the hill to eat from my grandmother's pots.

No one could make my father laugh like Uncle Joe. Poppy Tommy's only son born free, Uncle Joe, embodied that concept in his thoughts and actions. He had a freedom in his spirit that most Negroes did not

have. At times, it seemed that Uncle Joe did not understand the southern caste system that dictated our lives. I
used to hear my father say Uncle Joe did not know his
place. Even when my father said this to Uncle Joe, it
seemed as if he simply did not comprehend my father's
words. Uncle Joe was a kind man and he showed his
kindness to all people he came in contact with, whether
they were white, Negro, male or female.

In the summer of the year in which I turned
sixteen, my father and Uncle Joe went to the Baker house
to build kitchen cabinets. They worked in the house
several days and each night my father returned upset
with Uncle Joe for not heeding Poppy Tommy's warning. Uncle Joe was too friendly with Mrs. Baker. His
conversation was too long, his smile too wide.

The night before the job was to be completed, I
heard my father outside yelling at Uncle Joe. While at
the Baker home that day, Mrs. Baker had stepped up
onto Uncle Joe's ladder to show him an uneven area on
the surface of the wood cabinet. As she showed Uncle
Joe the problem area she lost her balance and began to
fall. Uncle Joe caught her, and then he fell to the ground
with Mrs. Baker in his arms. The two stayed in this
position a moment too long, and in that moment Mr.
Baker walked into the room. Without a word, he slowly
walked over and lifted his wife out of Uncle Joe's arms.
He then escorted his wife to the next room, holding her

from behind as if she had been injured. Uncle Joe and my father continued their work uninterrupted, but Mr. Baker's silence, concerned my father.

That night he argued with my uncle, accusing him of jeopardizing both of their lives. I've never heard such angry words spew from my father's lips. The tone, made me sit straight up in my bed as I listened to my father alternate from scolding to pleading. It sounded as if my uncle made several futile attempts to make the discussion light, but my father's anger continued to elevate to the point that the two seemed to have a brief scuffle. I looked out the window to find both men on the ground; my Uncle Joe's face looked distorted. Without his seemingly permanent smile, he looked like a stranger. He spoke softly, and grabbing my father's arm with both tenderness and desperation, seemed to try to comfort my father, but after a few minutes Uncle Joe began to ascend the hill and the worry in my father's eyes revealed that Uncle Joe's efforts had failed.

My mother was waiting for my father when he came into the house. They spoke in a whisper, and after a while I could only hear my father's voice; he was repeatedly telling my mother how much he loved her. "I love you Rose, I love you. . . . . I love you . . . . I love you Rose. . . ." I fell asleep with my father's words floating in my head.

The following day my father and Uncle Joe

arrived home just after noon. They had completed the Baker job early, which usually meant they would spend the rest of the afternoon outside our house talking and laughing and drinking lemonade, and relaxing. On this day they did not stop at our house, but went straight up to the hill. As I watched them disappear into the shadows, their bodies looked broken. There was an uneasiness about them and a palpable wedge between them.

I went outside and waited for my father. I sat on the rope that he had tied around a low branch on the large oak tree outside of our house. I did not swing. I sat on the knot at the end of the rope and let the wind move my body gently to and fro. I strained my neck around one side of the rope and stared at that place on the hill where the tree shadows were interrupted by the sun's light shining through to the earth. After a short time, the outline of my father's body appeared in the sun drenched opening on the hill, but only for a moment. In a flicker he was gone. Running, my father was running down the hill. Something was terribly wrong. When he reached flat land, he did not slow down, but accelerated, and with each stride it looked as if his long arms were reaching into the heavens, searching for an angel to bring down to earth to protect us. As he approached the house he yelled to me to get my mother and to go inside the house.

Instinctively, I called out to my two younger

brothers who were playing out back in the cotton house. Before running into the house I looked back at my father, whose news caused my mother to cover her mouth with both hands. My mother shook her head vigorously from side to side, then her limbs lost life, and she fell into my father's arms. My father hugged my mother's limp body as a child hugs her favorite doll, then he lifted her off the ground and ran toward the house with my mother in his arms.

Once she recovered, my mother quickly joined me in gathering the few items that my father instructed us to bring. My father was in the shed behind the house with my brothers collecting his guns and ammunition. It looked as if my father was preparing for battle, against what or whom I did not know. Once back inside, he barked commands at my brothers and me, but when he turned to my mother, he was calm. His voice tender, he said "Rose, its time." My mother obediently moved toward the door, but then she darted back to the room that she and my father shared. Before my father could go after her, my mother returned holding a small golden heart shaped locket that my father had given her on their wedding day. In the other hand she grasped the Holy Bible. My mother held the Bible so tightly that the tips of her fingers turned white. Her body was shaking, and I could feel her fear.

When my father saw the Bible in my mother's

hand, he stopped. The urgency of the situation seemed to fade away, and he gathered his family in the middle of our little home, and prayed for us. Just as my father was finishing his prayer, we heard his older brother, Willy, calling out to him. When my father opened the door I was startled by what I saw. My father's two older brothers were outside with their families. Each man had two mules that were packed just like ours. I looked at my cousins' bewildered faces, and knew that they were just as confused as I was. My Uncles, Willy and Heron, only paused long enough to help my father finish loading the heavy bags onto the mules, then they continued their procession up to the hill with my father's family now joining them in the rear.

Shortly after we arrived at my grandfather's house, men from all around the area began to gather on the hill—uncles and cousins, friends of my father and grandfather. They were all drawn to the hill . . . for a purpose. As the men walked around Poppy Tommy's house, strategizing on how to protect it, I was able to collect enough information to piece together what was happening to my family and why.

The story that formed from the murmurings around me was so disturbing it made my heart sink deep into the pit of my stomach. The men said that shortly after noon, the word began to pass among the Negroes that an angry mob was forming in town. The object of their fury was Joe Johnson. The story that was circulating among the white folks was as follows: Joe Johnson had attacked and fondled Mr. Baker's wife while working in the Baker home. Mr. Baker said that he saw it with his own eyes, and that he had to forcefully free his wife from Joe Johnson's lustful grip. He said that Bobby Johnson was right there and saw the whole thing, but didn't do anything about it.

The story was passed around from person to person for most of the afternoon, and with each description the details became more exaggerated, the acts more horrendous. Mrs. Baker was screaming for help as Joe Johnson groped her breast. Bobby Johnson laughed, as he held her down. Mr. Baker had to first pull Bobby Johnson off of Mrs. Baker, then pry Joe Johnson's fingers from her flesh. By the time dusk fell, the mob of white men and some women were convinced that a crime had been committed; a crime that was punishable by death.

Once my grandfather got wind of what was happening in town, he began to organize a mob of his own. He lived a life of submission and conciliation, not because he wanted to, but because he knew that he must do this in order to protect his family. He was always respectful to white folks, never caused any problems, and was always willing to lend a hand. Now he was infuriated by the thought that a mob was forming, initiated by a story that had been fabricated by Jay Baker, a man who grew up, and even played with Poppy Tommy's two youngest sons. He was sickened by the fact that Jay Baker's parents, most of the people in that mob, and Jay Baker himself knew that the Johnson boys were not capable of committing such heinous acts. But he knew and understood that none of this mattered now.

Life for a Negro after slavery was in some ways more perilous than during slavery. A slave was basically subject to one man's wrath, his master's. Any person who acted against a slave would have to answer to that slave's master. The master then was both an oppressor and a protector of the slave. Once slavery ended, the Negro was left to clothe himself, feed himself, secure shelter and protect himself—all within a climate that was hostile toward him. After slavery, the Negro was fully exposed to harsh treatment from *any* white person, regardless of age, wealth or station. Every white person was superior to every Negro person. Every white person could take the law into his own hands if he had been somehow offended by the words or actions of a Negro. And so, the Negro lived each day knowing that he might be tortured, maimed, or killed if he looked at a white man wrong, or stared at a white woman too long, if he appeared rude or obnoxious, if he did not tip his hat fast enough . . . if he was accused of murder, rape, shoplifting, drunkenness . . . if he crossed paths with the wrong white man or woman on the wrong day. All of these offenses, or the mere suspicion of such an offense, might call for the lynching of a Negro.

Now, a lynch mob had formed with the intent to kill Poppy Tommy's children. He had worked so hard, tried so hard, taken so much. He loved his family, lived for his family, and now he would die for his family. Realizing that confrontation was imminent, he said to let them come, but not without a cost to them. There would be bloodshed on both sides and both sides would mourn the death of someone they loved.

By night fall, we could hear the angry crowd in the distance. The women and children were huddled in the corner of a back room in Poppy Tommy's house. The fifty or so men that had assembled on the hill were strategically positioned outside of the house. Most of the men were on the front porch with Poppy Tommy, but there were also men on each back corner of the house, along with a couple on the sides. The house rested on large cement blocks, allowing several men to crawl under the house and lie on their stomachs to point their rifles toward the road.

The windows had been boarded shut, but from the back room we could see flickering lights moving slowly up the hill through a gap that formed between two pieces of wood nailed to the side window. As the mob approached, the house was quiet. The men, our protectors, moved around and made preparations without a sound. The only noise within the house was my grandmother's whispered prayers. The closer they came the louder the noise, shouting I think, but the words were unintelligible. Maybe they were not words at all, just garbled expressions of hate.

It seemed as if the whole room held its breath. Some of the younger children sobbed silently. The older children believed in the strength and determination of their fathers and grandfather, but they were also aware of the viciousness and the barbarism of a group formed to kill.

A month before in the neighboring town, a Negro man and his young son were lynched after the child ran into the path of a horse drawn wagon while chasing a cat. In the father's attempt to save his child, he ran into a white woman, knocking her to the ground. His concern was catching up to his child before the horse struck him. When the man turned in the woman's direction, he saw that she was still on the ground and a small crowd had begun to form around her. The man and his son never made it back to their home that day. They were stoned until they both lay unconscious, and then they were hanged. His young wife was pregnant with their second child and the Negroes in the town were outraged by what they considered this unprovoked violence. The story spread fast around the area. It was even reported in the newspaper. It was a topic of discussion among Negroes for weeks, and so most children who heard and understood the conversations knew that an angry group of white folks were capable of anything.

The older children fought the images that tormented them every time they shut their eyes, images of their family members hanging from a tree with their eyes bulging and their arms swinging beside their lifeless bodies. They fought the same images of themselves, just children, but still at risk of becoming the unfortunate victims of a lynch mob.

The crowd that had swelled to well over one hundred people spit venom at Poppy Tommy, who was waiting for them at the top of the steps leading to his house. When they were just a couple of yards from the house they called out to Poppy Tommy. "We're here for Bobby and Joe."

With control and conviction in his voice my grandfather looked into the eyes of the man who rolled the names of Poppy Tommy's sons off his lips with familiarity, and said, "You can keep on comin' if you want to."

As several men broke from the group and began to advance, dozens of men emerged from the shadows of Poppy Tommy's porch with their rifles cocked and aimed directly at the group. In an instant the hunters became the hunted. Shock and terror came over the pursuers' faces as they realized that *their* lives were in danger. What looked like a sea of men lined the porch on either side of Poppy Tommy. But there were more men and more guns. A wave of panic went over the group as they spotted the men lying underneath the house, all with guns, all ready to pull the trigger.

Poppy Tommy and the others waited intently to see what the mob would do. The men remained completely still, ready to defend my grandfather and his family, but also to defend themselves and their families.

The incidents of lynching as a form of southern justice had been growing, and Negroes began to feel that if they did not fight back, this would become the preferred method of punishment, and the Negroes' rights to trials in court—a promise made, but never fully kept—would forever be forgotten.

Although many of the men in the mob were armed, they were not prepared for gun battle. They were ready to shoot bullets toward the sky, or maybe into the corpse of a dead Negro hanging from a tree, but they were not ready to engage a group of armed men. After several minutes of silence, the mass reluctantly retreated.

Their frustration boiled over in the form of taunts, insults, and threats. We heard a woman's voice cry out "Cowards." Then a man's voice yelled, "Dead

Niggas." Then the most upsetting, we heard a man's voice declare "I see you John C." And with that we all knew that John C. Brown's life was now in danger. His willingness to shield and protect our family had put his own family in jeopardy. Still thirsty for destruction, the mob torched three houses on the side of the road that lead them away from the hill—our homes.

I was jolted out of my sleep by my mother's scream, "Dead, Dead, they're both Dead."

Then I heard my grandmother sobbing, "They killed my babies, go get them Tommy, go get them from Pine's Lake."

I thought I must still be dreaming. My father and Uncle Joe are safe. Poppy Tommy and the other men protected them. They scared the white folks off. My grandmother always talked about how white folks respected my grandfather, and tonight they showed it. They left his family alone. They burned down houses, that could be rebuilt, but they brought no harm to Poppy Tommy's family.

My brother grabbed my arm, hoping that I had heard what he heard, hoping that I could explain to him what was happening and what the screams meant. I went to the bedroom door and opened it enough to see my grandmother on the floor surrounded by my aunts, who were fanning her. My mother was beside them on her knees, rocking back and forth. I saw my grandfather enter the room, and then quickly leave again. I tried to remember what I heard in my sleep. . . *Pines Lake, Pines Lake, go get them Tommy.* I had to go to Pines Lake. I had to see for myself if my father was dead or alive. I comforted my brother and assured him that I would find out what was happening. Still in my gown, I slipped out the back door and escaped into the darkness.

As I laid on my back, I watched the movement of the pine trees. As the wind blew, the tops of hundreds of tall thin pine trees swayed to and fro as if instead of trees, they were delicate flowers, powerless under the force of a gentle breeze. The moon, full and white, reflected off the lake, lighting up the area, and illuminating the two bodies that hung motionless on the large oak tree beside the water. When I first saw my father hanging there, I tried to scream out to him, but my voice was silenced by the fear that the mob of white people was still out there, hiding behind trees, under rocks, and beneath the surface of the water, waiting to terrorize another Negro. Waiting to watch him fight for his life, then plead for his life. Waiting to watch his arms and legs flail around as he tried to loosen the ever-tightening rope around his neck; waiting to watch his arms fall stiffly to his side; waiting to watch a Negro die.

Too frightened to make a sound, I screamed silently until my body, overwhelmed with shock and grief, collapsed. When I regained consciousness, I remained on my back, unwilling to look toward the lake, focusing instead on the trees. The night was calm and peaceful, and I began to doubt my mind. Surely my father and uncle's dead bodies were not hanging on a tree several feet from me. My doubt and confusion triumphed, and I turned onto my stomach to look.

As I studied the vessel that had once housed my father's soul, I marveled at its beauty. I looked past the contorted expression on his face, beyond the bulbous eyes. I ignored the tongue that hung outside his mouth and rested on his bottom lip. I rejected the image in front of me; instead I looked deeper, and I saw my father. He was so handsome and warm. He usually had a smile on his face, and a laugh was not far behind. Just the sound of his laughter would bring a smile to the face of all those within earshot. Even when he wasn't laughing, his eyes looked as if he were. He was always teasing with us children or huggin' on my mother. He had special names for all of us. He called me Virgi, for Virginia; the older of my two brothers was LilBo, for Little Bobby; my baby brother was Jimbo, for Jimmy; and my mother, he called her Beautiful. On some days my mother did not feel beautiful, and she pleaded with my father to call her by another name. On those days he called her Beautiful twice as much. My mother's growing impatience seemed to tickle my father, and with each scolding from my mother, my father would open those big brown lips revealing a set of magnificently white teeth. His smile grew brighter and wider throughout the day, and despite my mother's protest, she remained Beautiful to my father. From the first day my mother and father met, she could not resist his charm. She said when my father entered a room he had presence. He was a tall lean man with coal black hair and skin to match. His skin was strikingly dark, as dark as the night sky that now served as the backdrop for his strangled silhouette.

Respect. Respect from a white man to a black man meant they would not force you to turn over your own child to a lynch mob. Respect meant they would not beat your child, or drag your child behind a horse before hanging him. Respect meant they would not cover your child with coal tar and burn him at the stake. Respect meant they would not shoot at your child's corpse after he gasped his last breath and life had left his body. Respect meant they would not bore holes into your child with corkscrews, or pierce your child's flesh with knives. Respect meant they would not cut off ears, fingers, toes, extract teeth, eyeballs, collect the bones of your child as a souvenir, a keepsake to remember the event, evidence of a job well done, a trophy to show off the accomplishment. Respect meant they would not castrate your child, removing that part of the Negro that they find most offensive and most threatening. Respect meant they would let you climb up the tree, crawl across that branch, and cut the rope that formed a noose around your child's neck, then watch your other two sons catch the bodies of their brothers before they hit the ground. Respect. My grandmother always said them white folks respected my grandfather.

More than a year after the murder of my father and Uncle Joe, our family remained devastated. My grandfather, once the proud head of his clan, was now broken and defeated. After several futile attempts to seek justice for his sons, my grandfather withdrew deep into himself. For much of the day Poppy Tommy would sit in silence, staring blankly into the distance, haunted by decisions he made on that fateful night, decisions that cost his children their lives. In his mind he replayed the night, rethought his failed plan to smuggle his children in a wagon transporting cotton to the next town. Should he have waited, been more patient, and allowed the furor to pass? Should he have killed those men and women before they had an opportunity to kill his children? Should he have known that they would still be out there waiting? These questions consumed him; the thoughts tormented him each hour of every day. The doubt and regret were parasitic, slowly sucking life from his spirit. His laughter that once resonated through every room of the house was now silenced. His words that nourished our minds and hearts were now lost. His work that once provided food and shelter for his family was nonexistent. He seldom spoke, and when he did, he was cross and irritated, the words angry and harsh.

We were not to speak of my father or uncle, not even mention their names. It was as if my grandfather wished to forget they existed, forget how he failed his family, and forget that he did not protect his sons. But they did exist, and my brothers and I were evidence of my father's life. It seemed as if my grandfather viewed us as constant reminders of his failure, and for that he resented us.

Suffering from the absence of my father, and feeling the rejection of my grandfather, my brother LilBo became angry and unmanageable. I, too, began to despise my grandfather. I refused to forget my father. At night just before I fell asleep and in the morning when I awoke I would lie completely still, with my eyes tightly shut, and I could see my father. I could see his smile, I could hear his laughter, and sometimes I could even feel his touch as he hugged me or held my hand.

My grandfather quickly stifled any verbal recollection of my father. Sometimes we were severely scolded, other times we were sent to fetch a switch for our beating. My grandfather did not work after the death of his sons. Although his carpentry skills were still sought after, he refused to enter the homes of white folks, not knowing if they had been involved in the lynching of his children. Because of this, everyone else in the family had to work.

My mother began to teach lessons to Negro children at a makeshift schoolhouse across town. Once soft spoken and sweet, almost fragile, my mother became hardened after the death of my father. This may have been due to the unexpected responsibility she now had of providing for her family. Maybe she was hardened by the constant ache inside of her that kept her from sleeping at times, and kept her from eating at other times. She may have become more and more hardened each day that she walked past the Baker house and saw Mrs. Baker's stomach swell. Month after month, Mrs. Baker made a special effort to say hello to my mother as she walked by the Baker house in the afternoon.

How painful it must have been for my mother to watch the woman who caused the death of my father, and all but took the life of my mother, giddy with the anticipation of new life, hopeful for what the future would hold for her and her family. My mother fought the bitterness that threatened to consume her by putting all of her energy into making a life for herself and her children.

After teaching at the schoolhouse, my mother taught piano lessons, then she returned home to join my grandmother and aunts on the porch where she helped them shuck corn, shell peas and snap beans for canning.

Since the murder of my father and uncle, it felt as if our family had a rope around its neck, slowly tightening and restricting our breathing, blurring our vision, challenging our desire to live. But on one particular afternoon the rope that threatened to kill our family was loosed, and we took our first deep breath in over a year. It was on this afternoon that our family reclaimed itself.

My mother, grandmother and aunts were on the porch making preparation for canning vegetables. My grandfather was also on the porch rocking back and forth on a stool, watching us children. My brothers and cousins were playing horseshoes in the dirt. I was sitting on the porch gathering the scraps of pea shells. While my grandmother had gone into the house to check on the peas boiling in the pot, my mother called out to my brother, Lilbo, to fetch the mason jars from the shed. My brother did not respond. My mother called out to him again, this time standing at the top of the porch steps. My brother defiantly waved his hand at my mother and began to walk toward the dirt road leading away from the hill. My mother slowly walked down the steps and calmly picked up a hardened clump of dirt from the side of the steps. As my brother, who never looked back, made his way toward the road, my mother chucked the clump of dirt in my brother's direction, hitting him squarely in the back of the head and knocking him to the ground.

We all stared silently as my brother stumbled to his feet. Then, the silence was broken by a roar, a roar of laughter from my grandfather. This sound was so foreign to all of us that it caused my grandmother to come bursting through the screen door, almost slipping and falling as she strained to see what the commotion was. My mother looked over at my grandfather, also startled by his outburst. But once she saw the smile on his face, she too began to laugh. Broken up by laughter Poppy Tommy belted out, "If Bobby could have seen that, we would have had to pick him up off the ground he be so weak from laughin'." With that my mother's laughter, now mixed with tears, grew stronger, and the laughter was infectious, even reaching my brother, who chuckled as he rubbed the bump that was forming on the back of his head.

On this afternoon my grandfather realized the inner strength of my mother and even borrowed strength from her. On this afternoon my grandfather stopped worrying about my mother, and his grandchildren. He recognized that she would do whatever it took to wrestle her family from the legacy of a lynching.

MIGRATION

3

MIGRATION

My mother held my hand tightly as we stood outside of Grand Central Station.

As the youngest child of my grandparents, Virginia and George, my mother, Pauline, was the first to make the move to the North. Having arrived safely, my sister was hoisted up on my mother's hip with her legs straddling my mother's body. I stood in front of my mother, resting the back of my head against her stomach, but never letting go of her hand. All of the grandiose thoughts of Chicago swiftly disintegrated as I watched the hundreds of people hurriedly shuffle past us. Some looked as if they would barrel into us, or each other, but amazingly, the bodies seemed to maneuver around the next, avoiding collision.

The air was thick and carried a peculiar smell. The streets were dirty. There was paper and even bottles on the ground. A few feet away from us laid a man whose hair was unkempt, his mouth was missing teeth, and his clothes were soiled and wreaked of urine. One man, while walking past us, and likely sensing our bewilderment, hollered to my mother "Hey Baby." Startled, my mother snapped at me, "Eva, stay close." Then she squeezed my hand tighter, and I did not know if she was comforting me, or I her.

The people looked busy, preoccupied, unfriendly, worried, and unhappy. Face after face, showed misery, struggle and wear. Then out of the sea of unfamiliar faces came my father. I will never forget how he looked on that day. He was the most handsome vision I ever laid eyes on. He was dressed in a beautiful black uniform, and wore a hat that had gold metal lettering on the front. His shirt was white and crisp; his shoes were black and shiny. He walked upright and proud. When he saw us he began to grin, and his smile melted away the cold that had lingered well past the thaw of the Chicago winter.

We must have been a sight to see. We had all been dressed in our Sunday's best, but now among the masses of the urbanized population, our clothes looked like field wear only fit for farming crops. My sister's shirt was a yellowish white and hung off of her shoulder slightly, a misfit hand me down of mine. And my dress and shoes were worn. The sleeves stopped just short of my wrists, and there was a tear at the hemline, which until this point had seemed too small to notice. My mother donned a floral church dress that she had had for as long as I could remember, but the dress was pretty, and now the still vibrant purple and orange flowers scattered throughout the dress made me feel a little bit of home in this foreign land. She also wore a hat that had always looked nice with the dress when we were down South, but now it looked out of place and outdated.

My father walked over to us with confidence, and I thought his shirt would burst open from the pressure of his chest. When he reached us we all hugged together, then he gave each of us a big kiss on the lips, starting and ending with my mother; the first on the lips and the second on my mother's protruding belly. And for the first time since stepping off the train, I felt that life away from home, away from the farm and away from family, would be all right.

My father had just ended a two-week shift and was off for two days before he would travel the train lines again. My father was a Pullman Porter, and our family was very proud of this. The descendants of slaves were lured to the North by the promise of a better life, better wages, and better treatment. Most worked in factories or in the stockyards, but those who became Pullman Porters truly achieved a level of success. The men chosen to work for the Pullman Company were good looking, finely built men. Their exceptionally well-maintained uniforms gave them a distinguished look, and their exposure to different places and different people gave them an air of culture that most colored people did not have. Pullman Porters were also some of the most well paid men around, because of the generous tips they received in addition to their wages. To be a Pullman Porter was a mark of prestige and distinction.

My father became a porter shortly after Pearl Harbor was bombed. The Pullman Company transported soldiers across the country, and there was a great demand for porters during this time. My father had been a porter for almost a year saving enough money to send for us. On one of his trips he came close to home and had been able to sleep at our house instead of at the boarding house with the other porters. Shortly after this visit, my mother realized she was pregnant, and my father decided it was time for us to start our new life as a family up North.

When we arrived at our house, I was amazed by its size. My mother told us that our father was making good money, and preparing a place for us to live once we came up North. But this house was beyond my greatest expectations. It was a large brick house with three stories. Leading up to the door were four wide cement steps with short brick columns on each side. Each of us would have our own room, I thought to myself, and there would even be room for Grandmother Virginia to visit.

When we left Mississippi, Mother Virginia, who spent most of her day rocking on the porch, smoking her corn-cob pipe, told my mother that she wouldn't be coming up to Chicago. If we wanted to see her we would just have to come back down South.

Mother Virginia was always talking about what she wasn't going to do; always taking her positions, which she usually stuck to. But after I saw the house I was sure I could convince Mother Virginia to change her mind and stay with us in Chicago.

Once inside the building, a short portly colored man ushered us into a large room right off of the kitchen. The room was empty except for a large bed against one of the walls. The man then showed us the kitchen and the washroom, giving detailed instruction to my mother and father about our movement in the house. My confusion grew as I continued to listen to the man talk. Why was he telling us how to behave? Why couldn't we see the other rooms in the house? After a short while we walked back to the room near the kitchen and the man left, shutting and locking the door behind him. My father then turned to my mother and us children and exclaimed with open arms and a proud smile, "Welcome Home!" My mother beamed at my father.

My parents knew each other since they were children, and my mother said my father had been talking about moving up North for as long as she could remember. This was his dream. It became their dream, and now he had secured that dream for them. They spent a year apart, a year of sacrifice in preparation for this moment. My mother reached both arms around my father's neck and kissed him on the lips, "You did it Clifford, you did it," she exclaimed.

My father smiled at my mother with contentment, then corrected her, "No we did it Pauline."

He had talked about moving up North since he was about ten years old, and my mother, who later became his wife, never doubted him. She never said he was foolish, like the other children. She never said he wouldn't last long up there, like the other teenagers. She never discouraged him from going North, ahead of his family to find work, like the other wives did. She always believed in him, encouraged him and now he proved to her that her unfaltering faith in him was deserved. With love and appreciation, my father lifted my mother off of her feet and spun her around. With hope and anticipation, my father and mother laughed as he lowered her feet back to the floor.

Then, with authority, my father repeated the instructions outlined by the stout stranger: Our family could use the washroom from 7-7:30 a.m. each morning to wash up. On Saturdays we were given an extended amount of time so that we could bathe in the tub. We were to eat our breakfast in the kitchen, but our dinner was to be eaten in our room, so that the people who ran the policy operation in the kitchen each night could set up.

The policy operation was a way that people made money in the city without working for it. Policy runners would approach folks in the neighborhood, asking if they had any numbers they wanted to play. The runner would record their number and the people would pay the runner. The numbers were actually drawn from the wheel each night in the kitchen of the flat where we lived; money would then be paid out to the people who chose the winning numbers. Because of the policy wheel there were always people coming and going, most of whom we did not know, and so we were restricted to our room after 8:00 in the evening.

On that first night, I laid on the small pallet that served as a bed for my sister and me, and listened to the night sounds. In early evening the house seemed very busy. The front door to the building continually opened and closed. There seemed to be a lot of activity in the kitchen, a place where we were forbidden to go after 7:00 p.m. As the night went on, the sounds changed. The house became quiet, except for the music that came from one of the second floor rooms. Outside, cats squealed, dogs howled, and at one point some people walked by talking loud and laughing.

These night sounds were so different from the night sounds down South, and I wished I could be back there, listening to the crickets chirp, and feeling the breeze that came through my window at night, fragrant with the sweet smell of the magnolia tree that grew right outside the window. I wished that I could be back there, eating Mother Virginia's sweet potato pie, and chewing on sugar cane, or sucking on watermelon rind. This place was cold and although I was in the same room with all of my family, I felt lonely and disoriented. My father and mother began moving around on the bed, and I closed my eyes tightly and fell to sleep.

We were awakened early the next morning, and began our daily routine, starting in the washroom and then moving to the kitchen to eat. My mother cooked breakfast from the food that my father had bought in preparation for our arrival; patty sausage and grits, just like home. The rest of our first day in Chicago was spent visiting friends and relatives from home that had previously made the journey up North. As we moved from place to place, I was disturbed by what I saw and how the conditions and lives of these new migrants contrasted with the stories about the North that had been shared with us before we moved. Most of the stories revolved around the amount of money people made, and how lavishly they lived, but what I observed was cramped living quarters, small food rations, and housing that did not seem adequate for a person to occupy.

My mother's cousin Willy B., who used to drive down South to visit us, always bragged about his life in Chicago and how sophisticated and cultured he was. Cutin' Willy B. lived in what looked like an oversized broom closet, and the car that he claimed was his, was actually borrowed from a friend. The clothes he wore when he visited must have been someone else's as well, because it appeared as if Cutin' Willy B. had two pairs of trousers and three shirts, none of them rivaling the wardrobe he showcased on his trips home. It seemed as if every possible space in these buildings was used for boarders, and I later came to find out that our building was no different.

When we first moved to Chicago, the people seemed unfriendly, even those living in the house with us. Everyone seemed to be in a hurry to return to his own room, only speaking in passing, and never stopping to have conversation. The air contained the remnants of a cold Chicago winter, and I quickly came to understand many of these movements. But a few months after we came up North, spring turned into summer and the city came alive. The street became active with children playing, and men and women standing around on the front stoop or at the corner store, talking, laughing, and relaxing. That first summer, we came to know the people who lived in our building. We were forced together by the summer heat. On oppressively hot days we would all escape to the front stoop, fleeing from the unbearable heat inside the building.

Ms. Leila lived right above us and she always had male friends coming to see her. She wore a lot of makeup and always smelled good. She was glamorous. Some days I would study her as she talked to men who passed by the building, then my girlfriends and I would try to imitate her. We always knew when she was alone, because she would come in and turn the same record on everyday, and we would hear, "Caldonia, Caldonia, What Makes Your Big Head So Hard?" This song played over and over again when she was alone, but when she had company, the songs changed, they were sweeter, more sultry and seductive.

Mr. Jackson lived in the basement. He had a band, and on Saturday and Sunday the band would practice down in the basement. Some of the children on the block would lie down on the ground and peek through the window and watch the band practice. Mr. Jackson allowed us to do this and even put on somewhat of a show for us as he sang or played his horn. Mr. Jackson's hair was slicked down real straight with a part on the side and sometimes as he would sing and practice his dance steps, sliding his hand over his shiny black hair, which always tickled the girls.

Mr. Sawyer was an angry old man who had lived in New York, Philadelphia, and Detroit, before moving to Chicago. Mr. Sawyer hated white folks just as much as they hated us, and most of his conversations included criticizing and blaming the white man for the condition of colored people in this country. At first, I thought his dissatisfaction was with Chicago, or maybe he didn't like living up North, but he frequently lamented that he should have made the trip to Africa, and it became clear to me that he did not even want to live in this country. His complaining was incessant, and on some days, when his rampage was particularly impassioned, I too wished he had made the move to Africa, so we wouldn't have to hear him complain any more.

Mr. Sawyer's preoccupation with white folks puzzled me, especially since they seemed not to exist in our world. One afternoon, while listening to Mr. Sawyer rant, I realized that other than the Grossmans, who owned the grocery store at the end of the block, I had not seen a white face since the day we came to Chicago. I leaned over to one of the older girls who also lived in the building and asked her where the white folks were. She explained that they lived in a separate part of town.

They had their neighborhood, and we had ours and that was just the way it was in the city.

Much of the movement of colored people from the South to the North was a result of the urgings of those who had already made their departure. The message conveyed was clear, Jim Crow don't live up North. The North was thought to be more sophisticated, and it was, right down to its bigotry. Segregation was alive and well in the North, concealed by a carefully devised invention called the urban ghetto. Outside of work, colored folks spent most of their life within a ten to twenty block radius. Colored people owned most of the businesses in the neighborhood, and interaction with white folks was limited. There was a clear division of the races in the North, but it was orchestrated in a non-offensive, non-obtrusive way, and colored folks were content, and white folks were content to share a city, but not a city block.

The summer of our first year in Chicago was also when I met the person who would become my lifelong friend. Rita Harris' family owned the building across the street from us. The whole first floor belonged to Rita's family, and they rented out four rooms on the second and third floors. Rita's father worked for the Chicago Transit Authority, and they seemed to have more money than the rest of us. At first, her family did not encourage our friendship and had very little to say to my parents. Maybe my parents seemed less sophisticated than Rita's parents who had lived up North since they were children. Maybe Rita's parents felt a need to make a distinction between themselves and the poor colored folks that lived around them, creating for them a caste system within the American caste system. Whatever the reason for her parents behavior, Rita and I were undeterred. We became inseparable friends during my first summer in Chicago, and that never changed. Through the years, Rita and I experienced many joys together, as well as disappointments, heartache . . . and punishments.

Rita became my refuge from a home filled with strife and discontent. My father went back to work two days after our move to Chicago, and it soon became apparent that he would be away from us more than he would be with us. Having not seen him but once or twice in the previous year, my sister and I adjusted to my father's absence, always anticipating his homecoming. My father's absence seemed to take the greatest toll on my mother. Several months after we moved up North my mother changed. She became angry and mean spirited, tense and guarded. She seemed afraid and overwhelmed by the new surroundings and her new responsibilities, which included a newborn baby girl.

At home, she had Mother Virginia to help with cooking, cleaning, and raising us. But up North she had to fend for herself without her mother, and without the protection and guidance of her husband, who was on the road more often than he was home. Possibly, in an effort to shield and protect us, my mother limited our movements. As the years passed, our activities were restricted. Outside of school, she would let us play out on the stoop and she also allowed me to play over at Rita's house.

We would enjoy some additional freedoms when my father returned home, but there was a great cost involved and soon my sister and I decided that the freedom was not worth the conflict it caused between our parents. From the moment my father left on a trip, we would anxiously await his return. My father was high-spirited and warm hearted, and when he returned, he would remind us that we were loved. After some trips he would bring back the outdated magazines that were provided for the passengers as they traveled through the country. We were always excited when we saw my father pull out old copies of Life or Variety magazines.

In later years, my sisters and I would read the magazines from cover to cover, and with each turned page we were exposed to a life outside of the twenty blocks that defined our entire world. We learned about Bermuda and Sweden; we saw how the movie stars lived in California, and the bright lights of Times

Square. We could imagine ourselves in those places, and even in the houses in the photographs. The magazines also cultivated in us a love for reading, and a love for learning.

For my brother, who was born almost two years after we moved to Chicago, my father always took him aside and told him additional stories about the places he saw and the people he met, some of whom were famous. My father would also give my brother two bits, from the tips he received from the generous and wealthy patrons on the sleeping cars.

The joy of my father's return was mixed with sadness. When my father returned home, the intensity of my mother's anger would escalate. It seemed that she blamed or resented my father, possibly for uprooting their family, possibly for his absence. My father was baffled by my mother's behavior. From the time they were married, the two had planned to migrate to the North. This was their dream for a better life for themselves, and their family.

Sometimes late at night when we were all expected to be asleep, I heard my father pleading with my mother to tell him what was wrong. She refused to tell him. I remember my father asking my mother if she still loved him. I held my breath and waited for her answer. Hearing the desperation in his voice, I was saddened that he might think she didn't. Sensing his longing to make everything right between them, I resented my mother for making him feel inadequate. But when my mother spoke, her voice was soft and tender; she said, "Clifford, I love you more than anything in this world." Unconsciously, I sat up to see if that sensitive woman telling my father how deeply she loved him was my mother. It was if my mother had buried her true self safely behind this hard shell that she developed to protect herself. But what did she need protection from? My father only wanted to love her, and so through the years he tried to hold on to those words, hoping they would sustain him, and allow him to manage his frustration, with the understanding that although my mother would not show her love, he still had her heart.

Beyond the four walls of our room, life was free and easy, especially after the war. The war brought money and jobs to colored folks, and although most families remained poor, people didn't really seem to mind. In the summer, the people on the block spent a lot of time together, sitting on the stoop, down at the corner talking, walking up and down the block. The girls my age spent most of those summer days jumping rope, playing hopscotch, little sally walker, and jacks. It usually did not take long for Rita and me to grow tired of these wholesome activities, and find some mischief to get into.

One afternoon, after proving to be able to jump the fastest and longest, I gestured to Rita to follow me. As I led her away from the jump rope, the girls continued to sing, "Mable, Mable, set the table, don't forget the red hot peas." As we walked around the side of the building where my family lived, the girls' chant became faster and faster as the girl jumping tried to keep up with the increasing pace of the twirling rope.

Although it wasn't the weekend, and we couldn't hear any music coming from Mr. Jackson's basement, we decided to look in Mr. Jackson's window to see if the band members were there. When we looked in the window we saw Mr. Jackson with Ms. Leila. They only had some of their clothes on and they were touching and kissing each other all over their bodies. Mr. Jackson was kissing on Ms. Leila's bare breast and she was holding and rubbing his head. Ms. Leila started to lift up her head, and before we realized that her eyes were closed, we ducked down low, fearing she might see us. But as we tried to lie down as flat as possible, so that no parts of our bodies were exposed, I bumped Rita's head, knocking it against the window. This alerted Mr. Jackson that someone might be at the window. "Who's out there?" he yelled, and with this we ran back to the front of the building and across the street to Rita's building.

Several weeks later, I was going outside to join a

game of double-dutch. Ms. Leila was coming down the stairs toward the door. I quickly ran out in front of her, and as I passed Mr. Jackson, who was talking to old man Sawyer, I mischievously taunted Mr. Jackson, "Yo girlfriend's comin' Mr. Jackson." Before he could respond, I was down the stairs and counting off to jump into the center of the ropes. Unsure of what I meant, he looked down at me with confusion, then quickly disregarded my words and continued his conversation.

A few days later, I sneaked around to the side of the building to show Rita I could smoke a cigarette, that I had found in Cutin' Willy B's jacket the week before when he stopped by to check on my mother. Just as I had finally gotten the cigarette lit, Mr. Jackson walked past on the sidewalk. He stopped and called out to me, "Eva, what you doing back there?"

"Nuthin' Mr. Jackson," I replied. But noticing that we were suspiciously close to his basement window, he persisted.

"Come on out from over there," he insisted.

"Yes suh," I yelled back, hoping this would suffice, and he would continue toward the steps of the building. But instead, he waited for a moment and then began to walk toward us. At first, I began to panic, but I did not want to throw the lighted cigarette on the ground, because I was afraid it would ignite the house or grass around it, and, because I feared I would be unable to relight it considering the difficulty I had previously. Rita glared at me. With her eyes she pleaded with me to drop the cigarette. But as Mr. Jackson approached, I was reminded that Mr. Jackson had a secret of his own.

Once he came close enough to see and smell what we were up to, he scolded me, "Gul, put that cigarette down!"

Taking the cigarette from behind my back, I was emboldened by the damning information I had on Mr. Jackson. With confidence I recanted, "I'll make you a deal Mr. Jackson. You don't tell my daddy about me smokin', and I won't tell my parents about what you be doin' with Ms. Leila down in the basement."

Mr. Jackson snatched the cigarette from my hand and stomped it out on the ground before walking toward the sidewalk and into the building.

I looked over at Rita with a half smile and a shoulder shrug, partially convinced that my threat to Mr. Jackson would keep us out of trouble. Mr. Jackson told my father about me smoking and he also told him that I was a peeping Tom, looking through his window and watching him when he had company. I never said a word to my father about Mr. Jackson and Ms. Leila, but I caught quite a whuppin' for my part, and couldn't hang out on the stoop with the rest of the children, including Rita, for over two weeks.

A couple of years after being in Chicago, my mother let me attend church with Rita and her family. For colored folks, Sunday church services were a celebration of our lives, our struggles, and our triumphs. We were taught to be thankful for what we had, and to be hopeful for what we did not have. Each Sunday the people would enter the church with the weight of their individual and collective burdens on them. But with each song, I watched the transformation of souls. I watched people, who were broken in their spirits, discouraged and disillusioned, become replenished.

The preacher's words fed them, rejuvenated them. No matter their condition, they praised the Lord, believing the words that flowed from their lips strengthened them and gave them the ability to face another day. When the people left the house of the Lord, they left renewed, with the armor of God around them, to protect them until they returned again for spiritual nourishment.

Each Sunday I watched the Lord change the downtrodden to conquerors, and I prayed for my mother, hoping that she too could know the power of God's love. But she refused my request to come to church, and I viewed her resistance, not only as a rejection of me, but a rejection of God.

The church was appropriately named PEACE, and although there were several words that completed the name of our church, it was simply PEACE to those who entered its doors. I longed for my mother to allow PEACE into her life, if only for a moment.

When Rita's family first began taking me to church with them, they seemed to view me as somewhat of a missionary project, bringing Christianity to the uncivilized heathen from the South, allowing me entrance into a church that on the whole, excluded new transplants from down South. But once I began attending church, I was drawn to it, and as the years passed I never missed an opportunity to experience and observe the power and influence the church had on people's lives.

When I was eleven years old, the Pastor began to call me Lil' Preacher. This stemmed from an incident that caused one of the most extreme punishments I ever experienced, but in the end, changed my life. In other words, as Pastor Paul would say, the devil meant it for evil, but the Lord meant it for good.

On a lazy summer afternoon when Rita's mother, Mrs. Harris, was at work at the phone company and Mr. Harris was off shift, we decided to help Rita's younger brother with a problem he was having. Rita's brother had sandy blondish hair. His hair contrasted with his brown skin, creating the appearance that he was always in need of a bath. Some of the children in the neighborhood called him dusty, or mudbug.

Some kids just called him sandy, which he disliked as much as the other names.

With Rita's mother at work, and my mother tending to my siblings, we came up with a solution to Rita's brother's problem. I went home and retrieved an old container of black shoe polish from the trunk where my father stored his porter supplies. I returned to Rita's house and we filled the container with a small amount of water, shaking the remnants of shoe polish free, and turning the mixture black. We rubbed the mixture on Rita's brother's head with an old sponge, dying his hair, and his forehead, ears, and the back of his neck. Shampoo seemed powerless against the dye, and Rita's brother had to sleep sitting up for a week while the dye faded.

After this incident, my parents forbade me from seeing Rita for a month, this included church. Missing PEACE, I decided to bring PEACE to our home. I became the preacher, the choir, and the usher. Each Sunday I would sing, letting my brother and sisters take turns shaking the old tambourine that Mother Young, one of the elder women at the church, had given me. I would collect offering, which was usually an old button, or a marble or a couple of jacks. Then I would preach, mimicking the pastor's words and imitating the pastor's movements and expressions. By the time I was allowed to return to PEACE, I was eager to show off my talents, and volunteered for any need the church had, especially those that entailed me speaking in front of the congregation.

As I grew older, my mother became suspicious of my every move. I was not allowed to date or go to any organized functions where there might be boys. The only place where my mother consistently allowed me to spend time was the church, and it became my escape.

When Rita and I turned sixteen, Rita began making plans to attend Roosevelt University to work toward a degree. My family did not have the money or interest in me taking classes at the University, and for the first time since Rita and I became friends; there was a clear distinction between my family and hers. There was a financial distinction, but more than that, there was a philosophical distinction. Rita's parents' philosophy cultivated growth and advancement. My parents' philosophy perpetuated poverty and stagnation.

In the summer, as Rita prepared to enter her first year of college, my resentment for my mother grew. Having overheard the argument my father and mother had when I asked them if I could enroll at Roosevelt University, I knew it was my mother who had finally convinced my father not to allow me to attend. One Sunday when I was to sing solo, I asked my parents to attend church with me, as I always did when I had a solo. My parents agreed to come to PEACE. Shocked and pleased by my parents acceptance of the invitation, I sang with more feeling than I ever had before, and when I finished singing, Pastor Paul called me down to the altar.

With uncertainty, I approached Pastor Paul. He placed his hands on my shoulders and turned my body so I was facing the congregation. Shortly after the Pastor began to speak, I realized that he was speaking about me; telling the congregation about my grades in school and my service in the church, and my love for the Lord. As I looked out at all of the people filling the pews, I remembered my impression of these same faces when we first arrived in Chicago, but now the scowls had been replaced with smiles. Some people, like Mother Young, even had tears streaming down their faces, but they were tears of joy.

The Pastor called my parents up to the front of the church. My mother remained seated, but my father walked up the center aisle and stood next to me as Pastor Paul announced that the church had been collecting money to send one young person to college, and the church had selected me. I enrolled at Roosevelt University that fall.

Our family had moved into a two bedroom apartment several years after arriving in Chicago.

When I was seventeen years old, my father, like most Pullman Porters, was able to buy a single family home for us. I think my father truly believed that my mother would finally be content after this move, but much to my father's disappointment, my mother's attitude changed little, and my father became impatient with her.

As a porter, he attended to every conceivable need of his passengers. He tried to fulfill all requests, no matter how big or how small. Always polite and courteous, he made himself available at all times of the day and night to assist his passengers. He greeted and received the passengers with a smile. He served them food and beverages. He made down and put away their berths with care and precision. He shined the passengers' shoes as they slept and made sure the passengers were not too cold, too hot, or uncomfortable in any way. He did all of this with a gracious disposition and a permanent smile.

When he came home he wanted to be cared for and loved. He wanted, for a moment, to be treated the same way he treated his passengers. He did not have the energy to cater to my mother's nastiness, or analyze her behavior. The move to our house was my father's final effort to reach my mother, and after this attempt failed he seemed to distance himself from her. I wished that we could go back down South, so my mother could be happy and my parents could find love in and for each other again.

But at the age of nineteen, through the death of a boy about two years older than my little brother Cliff, I learned what most colored people already knew. There was no hardship in the North that paralleled the oppression caused by southern white hatred. A boy, who lived several blocks away from us, was killed when he went down to Mississippi to visit relatives. His body was sent back to Chicago, and many people in the neighborhood went to his funeral. My parents did not allow us to attend the funeral, but when I heard the stories of the condition of his mutilated and mangled body, I cried, as if he were my own brother.

The death of one young boy jolted an entire nation of colored people. For those who had made the exodus out of the South, leaving family, familiarity and tradition, his death reminded them of why they *had* to leave the South, and why they would never call it home again.

Heaviness blanketed the community for many weeks after his death, and just as we began to rebound from his murder, devastating news reached Chicago. Returning home from a trip to the deep South, an assignment loathed by most porters, my father shared regretful news with a couple of men who were perched on the stoop. He reported that the men who had killed the little boy had been set free. When I heard this, I grieved again for the boy's mother and his family. How frustrated and helpless they must have felt. I wondered why they did not take the matter into their own hands, exacting justice on those men who killed their boy. Didn't his life matter? Didn't his death matter? The country said it didn't, but his mother let us know that it did. She did not allow colored folks to be complacent, to be desensitized, and despondent. Her child became everyone's child, and there was a collective mourning for his death.

The murder of that boy exposed America to the world. It exposed the South to the rest of the country, and it exposed the white southerner's resistance to the tides of change that had begun to grip the nation. And even as elusive justice so craftily escaped us, we waited, with guarded anticipation, and with diminished expectation. We waited for change. But as we waited, I like so many others, made a silent commitment, an agreement with myself that his death would not be in vain. My life would be a testament to his sacrifice.

That opportunity came shortly after his death. While walking past a student lounge on the college campus, I noticed that there was a group of colored students listening intently to a colored man. Dressed in a suit, this man was handing out pamphlets to the students. I quietly walked in from the back to hear what so interested the group.

The man was a representative from Meharry College. He was recruiting colored students to become medical doctors. I listened intently, and after the man finished talking, I eagerly moved toward the front of the room, waiting for my turn to speak to him. When he finally turned his attention to me, I breathlessly asked my first question, "Where is Meharry College?"

He brightly replied, "In Tennessee. Do you think you might be interested in coming to school here?" As he finished his question he handed me a piece of paper. "Everything you need to know is on this paper, including my address. Look it over, talk to your parents and we will be here waiting to give you the instruction you need to become a doctor and to help your people."

As I walked to the bus stop, I played back the man's words in my head . . . *help your people . . . become a doctor and help your people.* On the bus, and then as I walked home, I thought deeply about what I wanted to do. I was so thrilled by the prospect that, without thinking, I ran into the house and excitedly blurted the information out to my mother.

My mother glared back at me. "Did you say Tennessee? Yo daddy would never let you go live down South."

After my brother and sisters went to bed, my mother and I had a terrible argument. I told my mother that, together, we could convince my father to let me go. I just knew it. But she shifted her focus and asked me who I thought would feel comfortable going to a colored woman doctor. She told me it was time for me to have a job and make some money. I was working at the primary school near our house, but only part–time until I finished my degree. She felt it was time for me to have a job so that I could contribute to the house or find a place of my own. She told me to put those thoughts of becoming a doctor out of my head.

For all of my life I tried to be obedient to my mother, and on the few occasions, as I grew older when I did defy her, I did it secretly, and felt badly afterward. When I was fifteen, I asked my mother if I could take my little brother to the movie. Once we arrived at the movie theatre, I sent him in to watch the movie and walked down to the drug store to meet a boy that I liked.

Another instance when I was dishonest with my mother was on the night of my high school prom. Unaware of the date of the prom, my mother allowed me to sleep over at Rita's on prom night. Rita and I had transformed her Easter dress into a prom dress for me. Rita's mother fixed our hair, and even gave us flowers to pin on our dates. Before we left they told us how beautiful we looked, and Rita's father even told the boys how lucky they were to have us on their arms. I resented my mother for not experiencing this with me, but I remained quiet.

Even when I found my mother snooping around my room, looking under my pillow, under my mattress, and even smelling my panties—I don't know what she was looking for—the scent of a boy, I guess. I never protested. But now, I could not contain myself. Years of suppressed anger, hurt, and disappointment boiled up in me and I raised my voice at my mother for the first time in my life.

I told my mother, "I will be a doctor, you cannot keep me from this, you cannot hold me back Mama, you have tried to hold me back all of my life, but no more. Why can't you just love me Mama? Why can't you believe in me? Lift me up, don't put me down. Tell me I can do anything. But that's all right Mama. That's what I wanted for so long from you, to tell me you're proud of me, that I've grown into a beautiful young woman. But now I don't need that from you Mama, I had to find that from within. I tell myself, you can do it, Eva. Anything you want to do, anything you want to be, you can. And you know what Mama? I have finally convinced myself of that. And I will be a doctor, a colored woman doctor. I am going to help our people Mama. I am going to do this, and I want you and daddy's support. But if you can't give it to me, I will find some other way!"

My mother died when I was twenty years old, just two weeks before I would become the first member of our family to graduate from college. My father decided to take her back down South for burial. He said she was never the same once they moved up North, and he wanted to take her back home, where their life together had been tender and loving. My mother died of a heart attack at the age of forty-one and we were all in a state of shock as we made the trip back down South.

Late on the evening that we viewed my mother's body, the house was quiet. Most everyone was asleep, exhausted from the emotional exertion of the day. But my mother's sister, Aunt Belinda, and I were unable to sleep, so she made a pot of coffee. Between long periods of silence, we reminisced about my mother. It was as if we both wanted to say more than we were saying, but couldn't. Then I built up the nerve to say how I felt, "Antie, I really think the anger killed her."

My aunt looked away from me, and in a whisper she said my mother's name "Pauline," then as if receiving reassurance from out in the distance somewhere, she gave a long, labored sigh. Then she spoke softly, but with authority, "It wasn't the anger that killed her, Sugah." After a pause she continued, "It was the secret that killed your mother."

I looked into my Antie's eyes, unsure of whether I wanted her to continue, unsure of whether I could handle what she would disclose, unsure of whether the secret would further damage my feelings toward my mother. But before I could answer any of those questions, I heard my own voice, mixed with anger and confusion demand, "What Secret?"

My aunt slowly began to unravel a story that was painful for me to hear, and even more painful for her to tell. One late night when my father was traveling, my mother realized that she had forgotten her skillet in the kitchen that evening, before the policy wheel got started. When my mother first arrived in Chicago, she was suspicious of everyone, and extremely cautious in her movements. After having been in the city without incident for almost a year, she made a decision that went against her better judgment and the strict instructions of her husband. She locked the children in the room, and quickly went down to the kitchen to retrieve her skillet. On this particular night the landlord had set up a cot in the kitchen pantry and rented it out to a drifter for a night, which he would do from time to time. Keeping the lights off, so as not to disturb anyone, my mother felt her way around the kitchen, which was partially illuminated from an outside street light.

The man lying in the pantry watched my mother navigate the kitchen before grabbing her from behind and pushing her into the pantry and onto the cot. She had put a robe on over her gown before leaving our room, but the extra layer served for no protection, as the man, whose face she could not see in the darkness, and whose breath reeked of alcohol, lifted up her garments above her waist. She felt the sharp blade of a knife against her face, threatening to pierce her skin. The man told her if she screamed he would kill her, and she thought about the three children soundly sleeping in the next room, and so she kicked and she scratched, as the man violently penetrated her, but she never screamed.

As the man raped her, he held his lips close to her ear and breathlessly he whispered in a raspy voice, "You know you like this. Is this what you came looking for? I know you ain't got no man. You bin wantin' this ain't you? Ain't you?" Once his body stopped convulsing, he grabbed her neck and told her that if she didn't keep her mouth shut, he'd come back and kill her and whoever lived up in that room with her. With that, he removed his hand from her neck and shifted his weight just enough to allow her to slide from underneath him and stand to her feet.

Trembling she stumbled a few feet down the hall to our room, leaving the skillet behind. The man who raped my mother was gone before the light of day, and he took with him a part of my mother. After that night she was changed forever.

My father returned home from a trip two days later and my mother, still sore and damaged from the attack, let my father love her as he always did after a long trip. Too afraid to tell my father what had happened, and too afraid to risk becoming pregnant when it would prove impossible for my father to have sired the child, my mother endured the pain as she felt her fresh wounds tear open from the friction of my father's body moving inside of hers.

My aunt explained that my mother told her about the incident some ten months later, shortly after my brother, Clifford Jr., was born. "The thought that Little Cliff may not be your father's child ate away at your mother, and although she told me, she swore me to secrecy and I have never shared this with anyone until now. But I want you to understand who your mother was; she was not a woman incapable of loving, or full of hate and anger. She kept a secret that slowly poisoned her body, knowing that the revelation of that secret would not only destroy your father and brother, but the entire family. She loved you all too much to allow that to happen."

I pleaded with my aunt, "No, Antie, no."

My Antie grabbed both of my hands from across the table. As tears streamed down her face, she apologetically responded, "Yes, yes, yes."

Already emotionally drained, I deteriorated into uncontrollable sobbing. My aunt came around the table and hugged me from behind. She felt like my mother, and she smelled like my mother. I tightly squeezed her arms that criss-crossed in front of me, wishing she *were* my mother so I could tell her how much I loved her and tell her that I understood. Now, I would never have the opportunity to apologize to the woman who sacrificed so much of herself for her children; children, who in return judged and despised her.

Fighting the truth, I begged my aunt to tell me that I had misunderstood her; that she did not say what I thought she had said. I pleaded, "What do you mean, Antie? What do you mean?"

Her silence answered, saying "That is it. There is no more to tell," and signaling that the silence would now continue and this was never to be discussed again— not with her, and never with my brother or sisters.

We sat in silence long enough for my tears to dry. Then my aunt, confident that her point had been made, said in a comforting voice, "I wanna show you something." She went to the secretary in the next room, and returned with a letter. "I received this letter from your mother two weeks ago." I opened the letter and closely examined my mother's neat handwriting. "Start here, read it aloud," my aunt said as she tapped her finger on the letter.

Eva has been talking to Cliff and me about medical school. I have tried to discourage her. I told her there ain't no place for a colored girl to be a doctor. Who would go to her, feel comfortable with her? She has been teaching a science class at the primary school behind our house and I was hoping she would stay there after she graduates from college. B, she wants to be so much more than we are, and I just don't want her to get hurt. But you know she's just like Mama, determined and strong willed. Last night we had a terrible argument and I lay in bed all night thinking about what Eva said, why she wanted to be a doctor, why she knew she could do it, who she would help. I prayed to God throughout the night to give me guidance. I stopped reading and looked up at my aunt, shocked and surprised by my mother's reference and reliance on God. My aunt closed her eyes tightly and nodded her head several times, confirming my mother's faith and belief in God. With renewed understanding of my mother, I continued to read. *This morning I awoke and knew what I needed to do. I've decided to use the money that we are expecting from Mama's land, and pay for Eva to go to medical school. She believes in herself B, and I want her to know I love her and believe in her too. Can you imagine Eva a doctor?*

My aunt said the last words along with me, and when I looked up at my aunt through tear blurred vision I saw my mother reassuringly and lovingly smiling back at me.

The next morning, we laid my mother to rest, and as her coffin was lowered into the ground, I said farewell, knowing and understanding, forgiving, and loving my mother.

WAR

4

WAR

My mother pulled my hair tightly as I squirmed around on the floor in front of her.

She meticulously weaved sections of my hair together into plaits, careful not to miss one hair. Occasionally, I whimpered. Each time the coarse bristles of the brush made contact with my scalp, I winced and pulled away, but my mother's grip on my hair was so tight that this small movement did nothing to ease the pain. This was our Saturday evening ritual, and my mother always let me know that this was as much of a chore for her as it was for me. She easily grew impatient with my complaints and often warned, "Dorothy, if you don't stay still I'm gonna let you do your own hair." This was the threat that I received every Saturday, if I did not stop squirming, jolting, wincing, whimpering, and most of all screaming.

On one Saturday in the late fall of 1965, we started the ritual early. The day began as most Saturdays did, with my family members doing our chores around the house. My mother was vacuuming, I was dusting and my brothers were cleaning their room. My father was fixing my bedroom door that had begun to stick, making it impossible at times for me to get into or out of my room. Around noon, the phone rang and my father, attempting to be heard over the vacuum cleaner's rumble, yelled to my mother, "Eva, they'll be here in about three hours." My mother turned off the vacuum cleaner and, to my regret answered back, "Good, that gives me plenty of time to do Dorothy's hair."

My father had received orders that his battalion would ship out to a place called Vietnam. Not knowing when he would leave, my father's brothers, Uncle Bill and Uncle John, loaded up their families and made the drive from Illinois to California with hopes of seeing their brother before he shipped out. After caravanning for three days, my uncles, aunts and cousins were expected to arrive late Saturday afternoon. When they finally drove up we ran outside to greet them. My Uncle John was the oldest, and he and Aunt Patsy had two boys and a girl just like us. John-John was 14, Paul was 10 and Cheryl was 7. Uncle Bill was the youngest, and he and Aunt Lorraine had two little girls, Valerie, who was 5 and Veronica, who was 2.

Before going inside, we asked our parents if we could go down to the park. The answer was yes, for everyone but Veronica, who was too young. John-John was put in charge of Valerie, and the pack of us walked down the block with Valerie happily riding atop John-John's shoulders. While we played at the park, my father and uncles spent time alone talking on the patio behind our house, and then they hopped in the car and after some time returned with bags of food and drinks. Shortly after their return, my father's friends, all of whom were also waiting for word of when they would deploy, began showing up at our front door with their families. The atmosphere was festive. The men were excited. They were well-trained warriors; ready to battle whatever enemy was waiting over there for them.

Our parents had their drinks; there was plenty of food, laughter, and wild dancing. After we had eaten, the kids gathered into my brothers' room and made up a routine to *My Girl*, by the Temptations, and the Supremes' *Stop in the Name of Love*. Sharon Johnson and Leslie Robinson, two girls my age, swooned over my cousin John-John. They decided that we three "Supremes" should direct the song toward him. Seemingly uncomfortable with this unsolicited adoration, he politely declined, but after several minutes of their incessant prodding, he sheepishly agreed.

We put on a show for our parents who enthusiastically looked on, clapping, snapping and cheering as we displayed our synchronized dance moves. After we treated our parents to an encore performance, my father started playing his favorite records, and the whole house grooved to the real stuff. First Etta James belted out, "Somethins' got a hold on me yeah!!! Oh it must be love!!!"

As I danced in the corner with the rest of the kids, I looked over at my father and he winked and pointed at me just as the background singers declared, "Oh, it must be love!!" And I knew he loved me, and the excitement of being loved by this man caused my feet to leave the ground. I found myself jumping to the beat of the drums.

After several songs, my father walked over to the record player and before he played the next song, he dedicated it to my mother. Then he put the needle down on the wax and Marvin Gaye began to croon, "How Sweet It Is to Be Loved by You!" My mother's face lit up and she walked, on beat, over to the middle of the makeshift dance floor and fell into my father's awaiting arms.

After the children were sent to bed, the music changed. It was slower, softer, but powerful. The adults paired off and seemed to each enter a world of their own. There was no more loud laughter, or slappin hands, no more strut, walk or jerk. Each man now turned all of his attention to the woman he loved, and for each couple it was as if no one else was in the room.

My mother and father talked and laughed as they gently rocked in each other's arms. Each time my mother looked into my father's eyes it was as if she was falling a little deeper in love with him. I stared, mesmerized by the sight. My mother was so beautiful, my father so strong, their love so deep. As I watched them, I felt special. I felt whole and safe. I was the product of this love, and I felt fortunate. As my mother placed her head on my father's chest, she glimpsed me peaking through the cracked bedroom door. Intoxicated by the moment, my mother tenderly smiled at me then slowly closed her eyes and let the music transport her to a private paradise where she and my father would live in this moment forever.

My mother and father met on the El train in Chicago shortly after my mother graduated from college. My mother was planning to study to be a doctor, but after her mother's death she put her plans on hold in order to help her father take care of her younger siblings. She decided to stay in Chicago and teach at the school behind her family's house.

Before the 1956 school year, my mother, still

interested in medicine, signed up for a week long seminar on nursing being held downtown. On the first day
of the seminar, she boarded the El train, found an
empty row of seats, and sat down in the seat closest to
the window. The train made two stops, and then on
the third stop, my mother could not help but notice a
handsome man who had entered the train dressed in a
military uniform. The man, in his crisp uniform and
perfectly shined black shoes, reminded her of her father in his porter uniform.

Upon boarding the train, the man passed several empty seats and sat down in the seat right next
to my mother. The man was high-spirited and jovial
and instantly struck up a conversation with my
mother, whose virtual silence did not seem to deter
him in any noticeable way. He held a lively conversation with my mother for almost a half an hour as the
train sped above the city.

Outwardly, my mother showed a lack of interest, remembering her mother's warnings about strange
men, but internally she was captivated by the man's
energy, and she rushed home after her seminar to tell
her friend Rita about the handsome stranger she met
on the train.

The next day, with no place to go, my father
boarded the same train, at the same time, hoping to
see the same woman. When he boarded the train he

was thrilled to see the woman sitting by herself looking out the window. He walked right up to the vacant seat as if she had beckoned him over to a seat she was saving for him, and sat down. Without hesitation, the twosome launched into conversation, and as the train sped along the tracks toward the woman's destination, my father watched her eyes sparkle as she told a story, and her top lip curl up when she smiled. He noticed that she used her long thin hands to express her thoughts, and she looked deep into his eyes when he spoke.

Enthralled in conversation and each other, the couple did not realize that the train had come to a stop. When the woman saw the name of the station, she jumped up frantically, and whizzed passed my father toward the open door. My father jumped up as well and nervously called out to her, asking her name. As the woman stepped off the train onto the platform, she turned to look over her shoulder, and with a sweet smile replied, "Eva!"

For the next three days my father "paid his fare, to share her air," as he liked to say. On Friday, the last day of the seminar, fearing he might never see my mother again, my father asked her out on a date.

Before the death of her mother, she would have quickly declined the invitation, unwilling to subject herself, or the nice young man, to her mother's irrational antics. But with a new found freedom, my mother accepted the invitation and spent the next Sunday afternoon with him at Washington Park. My mother's friend Rita says that they have been inseparable ever since, marrying just three months after meeting each other.

I gazed at my parents as they embraced, wondering what life would be like without my father at home. How would my mother cope with his absence? We never thought of losing my father. He was strong, indestructible, invincible. He squashed any fear we had about the possibility of him never returning. Even with this reassurance, I could not understand why my father had to leave us to fight a war far from home, when there were battles raging on the streets of America daily.

Just months before my father received his orders, the city of Los Angeles burned it seemed for an entire week. Each night we turned on the television to witness police and guardsmen clashing with a segment of the black population who chose a path that few blacks had chosen in the history of this country. They decided to declare war on the establishments that represented white dominance and oppression. They warred against the injustice of the justice system, the inequality of the economic system, and the deceit of a social and political system that promised them change with patience, obedience, faith, compliance, conformity, trust, and understanding.

I did not understand why it was so important to protect a people whose faces we did not recognize, whose names we did not know. Why were we willing and eager, to fight for, die for the cause of democracy outside of America's borders? Who was willing to die for democracy inside of America? Why was *their* freedom more important than ours? Why couldn't we see that the enemy from within was much more formidable than the enemy across the water? As the news depicted, night after night, in city after city, North and South, this enemy threatened to slowly destroy our nation. In Philadelphia, in Chicago and Los Angeles, race riots threatened to drive a deep, irreparable wedge between black and white America.

For black children, the images of other black children being knocked off their feet by the force of water from a fire hose made it easy to despise the South. Images of a black man's pants being ripped from his body by a dog whose leash was in the hands of a white policeman made it necessary to distrust the police. And images of burned out buses, and beaten Freedom Riders made it natural to hate white people.

It was under these conditions that I found myself traveling down South to stay with my mother's Aunt Belinda and her husband, Uncle Al, for the month of

July. My younger brother, Julius, stayed in California with my mother. But while my father was away in Vietnam my mother needed the support of her family, and Aunt Belinda offered to keep my older brother Gregory and me in Mississippi for what was sure to be four long weeks. It was there, in the deep South that I learned my greatest lesson about white people . . . about people.

Uncle Al and his brother drove to California to take my brother and me back to Mississippi. All I knew of the South was what I had seen on the television, and I could not understand why my mother would send us to such a wretched place. My confusion turned to outrage the day we began our journey to a world as foreign to us as the place my father had left for almost eight months earlier.

In the morning on the day of our departure, my mother called my brother and me into her and my father's room. She sat us on the bed and told us a story of a little boy from her neighborhood in Chicago who had gone to Mississippi to visit relatives. She explained to us that being black in the South was different than in California. There were rules we would have to follow. She instructed us not to speak to a white person unless spoken to, and then to speak with respect. She told us not to play with any white kids unless Aunt Belinda said it was all right. She emphasized to my brother that it included any type of ball playing.

At nine, my brother was becoming quite an athlete, and he was always eager to show off his skills to any willing victim. My brother looked puzzled. My mom, unwilling to take a chance on my brother disobeying her called his name, "Gregory, do you understand?"

My brother shrugged his shoulders and weakly answered, "Yeah."

My mother repeated, "Gregory, do you understand?" This time my mother paused for several seconds between each word, and Greg and I knew that this directive was different than any we had received in our young lives, and our reluctance to spend the summer down South was replaced with dread.

Once my mother made herself clear, we stood in the center of the room, held hands and prayed. Then with a mixture of fear and anger, my brother and I headed for the battlefield, just as my father had several months earlier.

Aunt Belinda worked for the Bailey family. She had worked in their home for much of her adult life, arriving at their house each morning just before dawn and spending the day cooking, cleaning and washing for Mrs. Bailey. This routine did not change while we were visiting, and much of our time in Mississippi was spent with our older cousins. Aunt Belinda did not have any children of her own, but she and my grandmother Pauline, had two brothers who with their families, lived close by.

Our cousins, a couple of whom had been bitten by the revolutionary bug, told us sensationalized stories about the white people in Mississippi; and with each story my heart hardened toward them. They also told us stories about President Kennedy, who was killed because, as they claimed, he tried to help black people. Only five years old, when he was killed, I remembered very little about his death, but our cousins told us that black people loved this President. They felt he was making life better for blacks in America, but he was killed before he was able to finish. One of my cousins told us that both of her parents wept at the news of the passing of the President. Another cousin recounted the reaction of the people in the neighborhood where he lived. He said everyone came out of their houses and stood around hugging and comforting each other, as if a friend or family member had been gunned down. When John F. Kennedy was killed it seemed as if the entire country paused, stopped, and mourned the loss of their leader, but for black people, they also mourned the loss of hope, and the optimism that died with the assassin's bullet.

My aunt returned from the Bailey house each afternoon around 3:00 p.m., and would begin the chores necessary for the maintenance of her own household. One afternoon after Aunt Belinda had returned from work, she called for me to help her remove the dry clothes from the clothesline on the side of the house. I walked behind her, holding a basket as she pulled sheets from the line and placed them in the basket. As I followed my aunt, I stared at her, amazed by her energy. *She must be tired*; I thought to myself, *she shouldn't have to work so hard.*

Then reflecting back on my cousins' stories, I became angry at those white people for misusing and mistreating my aunt. I thought, *Why should she clean their toilet bowls, and sweep their floors? Why should she be there at that woman's beck and call?* As feelings of disdain and disgust bubbled up inside of me I glared at my aunt's back, and with defiance I demanded, "Why do you work for that old white woman?"

My aunt spun around to face me, and bent down so that we were eye to eye. She pointed her long finger so that it was just short of the tip of my nose, and responded, "Let me tell you somethin' about that *old* white woman. That white woman's husband gave your Uncle Al, and my brothers, Ray and Frank their carpenter's licenses. He was the only white man in the county who was willing to give them papers which allowed them to support their families. That white woman's husband gave your Uncle Al the materials to build this house that you are stayin' in right now. When we got ready to sell some of Mother Virginia's land that was handed down from her grandfather, that white woman's husband paid a fair price for the land. When black people were being taken advantage of all over this area, he came in and paid us what the land was worth. And do you know what we did with that money? Your mother took part of that money and went to nursing school. She saved the other money for her brother and sisters to get an education. They all took college classes and Uncle Cliff graduated from college. That money served the same purpose for Uncle Ray and Uncle Frank's families. That white woman always asked about your mother and her sisters and brother after your grandmother Pauline passed away. Several times, after I would tell her how well your mother was doing in school, or how Cliff was trying to take summer classes, Ms. Bailey would stuff a wad of money into my hands and put her finger over her lips and whisper 'Shhhh.' Then she would smile and squeeze my hands. That money helped your Aunts Carol and Janice open up their beauty shop, helped your mother buy her books, and helped your Uncle Cliff sign up for his summer programs. That old white woman and her husband are friends of this family, so I don't want to ever hear somethin' like that come out of your mouth again!"

Ashamed, I dropped my head, and staring at

the ground, softly apologized to my aunt.

Growing up in the military, there was not much talk about differences, instead we were taught to unite behind our president and under our flag. But in this climate full of white racism and prejudice, black resistance and protest, the ignorance that divided the races seeped into my bones, and I found myself frustrated, confused and unsure of where to direct these emotions.

It was in rural Mississippi, off of a narrow dirt road, in a house my uncles built, without teacher or books that I learned one of the greatest lessons in my life from a woman with no more than a fifth grade education. It was there that I learned that goodness in people was not determined by skin color.

I headed back home with a clearer understanding of myself and this world, and as I stared out of the window of Uncle Al's car, I silently thanked my aunt for her wisdom and for her ability to pass it on to me.

My father returned home shortly after the new year, and with my father home safe, and the war a world away, my brothers and I pretended as if we did not see the marshal cars driving around the neighborhood; didn't hear about the death of another schoolmate's father. But this fantasyland we created came crashing down in February of the year that I would turn ten years old.

The end of life as we knew it began late on a cold wintry night in February when I awoke to my father's tirade. At first I thought my parents were having an argument, but then my father cursed, which I had never heard him do before. I heard my mother pleading with him to lower his voice, which he did, making it difficult for me to hear what had made my father so angry. I crawled out of bed, and tiptoed to the door. I quickly realized that my mother was not the target of my father's profanity. My father's rage was directed at the newsman for seemingly taking a position earlier that evening, against the war.

Maybe the newsman just echoed what many Americans felt after the media broadcasted disturbing images of dead American soldiers being drug around the embassy in Saigon. But to hear doubt in the voice of a man, who most Americans trusted and revered, was devastating to my father. He knew all too well how desperately the soldiers in Vietnam needed the support and understanding of those they had been sent to represent. My father continued to seethe and I quietly crawled back into bed, sorry that I had ever gotten out. As I stared sleeplessly at the ceiling and thought about my father's words, I came to realize, but not to understand, that his reaction was personal.

The next morning, I braced myself for the worst, but we were told nothing. Two days passed without incident and I breathed a sigh of relief. On the third day I ran home from school ahead of my brothers, who remained outside in the front yard playing ball. When I entered the house, I heard my mother crying. I associated my mother's tears with my father being away, and I became disoriented, *Was my father O.K.? Had he been killed in Vietnam?* I dropped my school bag and ran to the kitchen to see what was wrong.

When I reached the kitchen, my father was sitting right there in front of my mother. At first, the sight of my father gave me relief, but then I noticed that my father had also been crying, which I had never seen him do. This terrified me. As tears began to well up in my eyes, I pleaded, "What's wrong?" My father looked up at me and with a defeated tone, told me to go get my brothers. Frantically, I ran to the front, whipped open the screen door and yelled to my brothers to come inside. With no acknowledgement of my command, my older brother cocked his bat, and my younger brother wound up for the pitch. "Daddy said," I yelled. With this, bat, mitt and ball fell to the ground and they ran into the house after me.

Choking back tears, my father informed us, "I have received orders," and with pursed lips he paused and took a deep breath, "I must return to Vietnam." My father said the words as if he had received a death sentence. My mother sat in a kitchen chair, sobbing, seemingly certain that this war would make her a widow. My older brother wrapped his long arms around my father's neck and cried.

In an instant I was reminded of the marshal cars that drove through our neighborhood now, almost on a daily basis, cars that I tried to ignore, cars that symbolized death and loss. As I began to calculate the number of marshal cars I had seen, my entire body began to tremble. Dizzy, I stumbled backward just before my father's arms engulfed me. Safe, I nuzzled into his stomach, and the faint scent of his cologne soothed me as I pushed away thoughts of never seeing him again.

My father was gone within two weeks, reluctantly returning to Vietnam, in the year that would prove to be the deadliest for American troops.

Shortly after my father left, my brother began coming home from school with various injuries. First, he had a swollen nose, then a small cut beneath his eye. My mother did not notice at first, but one afternoon my brother returned home with a black eye. With a combination of anger and concern, my mother demanded to know what had happened.

My brother told my mother about the protesters that we saw when we walked to school. He told her about the kids in school that would taunt the military children and call our fathers nasty names. He told her about the boy that he had been getting into fights with, a boy whose older brother had just received his draft card, a boy whose family was enraged at the possibility of losing their son, for a cause that none of them understood or cared about.

As my brother spoke he began to cry. My mother rubbed his back and comforted him. I looked over at my brother with envy. I envied him for being able to take his anger and frustration out on someone. I envied him for being able to cry because of a busted lip or a black eye. I envied him for having a physical justification for his tears. With nowhere to direct my fear and anger, I held it inside. My tears were shed in the wee hours of the night, when everyone was asleep, and the house was quiet. In the predawn stillness I would lie awake, trying to make sense of what I saw in a country that seemed to vilify the very men who risked their lives daily, and lost their lives daily for their country.

In the darkness, my father's absence resonated throughout the house. It was then that I missed him the most. When my father was home the house felt alive, warm, secure, peaceful. But with him away, the house felt empty, fragile. I felt unsafe and vulnerable, and these feelings were heightened in April of the same year, with the murder of Martin Luther King, Jr.

After the violent death of our nonviolent leader, blacks erupted into violence. Blacks across the nation watched their women and children attacked by dogs, beaten with billy clubs, and overpowered by water hoses. We had experienced the murder of another black leader, Malcolm X, and of John Kennedy, a President who seemed committed to bringing equality to blacks, and then his brother, Robert Kennedy who seemed to share the same heart, and the man gunned down in Mississippi in front of his home, and the four little girls in the church in Alabama.

Blacks had sat by and watched their men be spat upon, and their young people have milk and sugar poured over their heads. Now, with the death of Martin Luther King, Jr., many blacks rebelled. They rebelled against a country that was created without ensuring the rights of all people. They rebelled against white people for their bigotry and hatred. And they rebelled even against the slain civil rights leader for making them believe that his strategy of civil disobedience and nonviolent protest may finally lead to equality for black men and women. They resented him for convincing them to love the people who had perpetrated such horrors on their own, love them that hate us, and love will prevail. Fed up and betrayed, the news of Martin Luther King Jr.'s death incited riots throughout the country. For many people, his death proved his dream a fallacy. In several cities, groups of blacks lashed out at anyone white, or anything that represented white power.

The day after Dr. King was murdered; my mother overheard my brother and a couple of his friends making plans to go over to an all white area about ten minutes from where we lived. Their plan was to jump the boys who lived there. With all of the force and conviction my mother could muster, she swung open the screen door and told the startled group, "You can go over there if you want to, but don't think they won't be waiting for you. Don't think that they won't be ready to fight." My brother tried to interrupt, but my mother continued talking, "So you make sure you are ready to get hurt, and maybe even killed today."

The boys stared at my mother in silence.

She stormed back into the house, partially shutting the main door, and standing behind it, hoping that the boys would heed her warning and stay put. She stood there, out of sight for almost five minutes, hoping her words were enough, but knowing that if she had to, she would physically stop my twelve year old brother from leaving the house.

While my father was gone, my mother had to play the dual role of both father and mother. She had to balance her natural tendency to be loving and nurturing with the necessity of being forceful and unbending. My father ran his house like a drill sergeant, and so my mother had not been involved much with disciplining us. But now she attempted to disguise her obvious un-preparedness, and maintain control and order in her home, while everything around her seemed to be in chaos.

With my father thousands of miles away, my mother discovered strengths and convictions within herself that she never knew existed. My brother tried out for the football team in our neighborhood while my father was gone. After several practices he had come home upset. He did not say anything to anyone when he walked in, and headed straight up to his bedroom. When my mother went upstairs to check on my brother he looked as if he had been crying. This time he had no noticeable bruises, but there was internal, emotional bruising. My brother had not been chosen as quarterback, a position that he had played before, and a position that he was clearly best suited for in comparison to the other boys on the team. When my brother told my mother the names of the two boys who had been chosen for the position she knew what was going on, and was sorry that her son had to have this experience.

There was no anger like the anger felt when a person has been purposely treated unfairly or discriminated against. His tears were tears of frustration. He knew he had been treated wrongly, but there was nothing he could do about it. They asked my brother to try out for quarterback, and he went up against the other two boys. Through his performance he proved that he was the best of the three boys, but when the decision was made, he was not selected, but the other two were. His spirit was crushed. He had not yet learned the skill that so many blacks found necessary to cope. He did not know how to reason and rationalize in order to give him clarity and peace of mind. He was still pure, believing that the nature of man was good.

My mother would not allow my brother to become disillusioned or discouraged, so with a mix of compassion and candor, she spoke to him. "You're gonna have to work twice as hard to get half as much."

My brother began to object, "But that's not fair."

With a quick rebut, my mother informed him, "It doesn't matter if it's fair. If that is what you have to do in this world to make it, then that's what you're gonna do." This was a lesson that she wanted all of her children to understand, so knowing that my younger brother and I were right outside the door eavesdropping, my mother turned her head toward the door, getting a quick glimpse of us before we darted out of sight, and said with confidence and resolve, "Dorothy, Julius, I hope you two heard that."

Our giggles revealed that we were in earshot, and that was enough for her. She knew that, unfortunately, she would have plenty of future opportunities to drive this point home, opportunities with each of her children.

My mother did everything in her power to stabilize us in my father's absence, but as the months passed, we became weary and exhausted with worry. Each day that we did not receive an early morning or late night knock on the door, each afternoon that we did not receive a visit from the "death patrol," as we began to call it, was considered a good day.

We prayed, hoped and persevered through 345 "good" days, but all of that came to an end on the 346th day.

It was a Saturday morning and I had spent the night before at a friend's house. I jumped down the front steps and landed on the sidewalk that would lead me three blocks toward home. I looked up from the sidewalk in time to catch the tail end of one of the big brown cars that we had become accustomed to seeing weave through the streets of this largely military neighborhood. The death patrol was at it again, and with my father gone now for almost a year I learned not to be immediately alarmed by the sight of the brown sedan. But this time it was different. It was different because the car was headed in the direction of my house.

At first I walked down the sidewalk slowly, trying to act as if I did not notice the car. Then the car made a left turn toward my street. Unconsciously, I began to run. Trying to keep up with the car, but frightened of being detected by the driver, I stayed on the next block and ran in the same direction, looking between the houses that I passed, never losing sight of the car. The car then made a familiar right turn and I bolted through the backyard of a house and on to the street that the Provost Marshal had just turned off of. Apparently confident of his whereabouts now, the driver sped up and I was unable to keep up with him.

When I finally turned the corner on to my street, I felt like someone had hit me in the stomach with a sledgehammer. I buckled over, and then fell to the ground. The brown car was parked half way down the street, directly in front of our house. As I tried to pick myself up, my body lurched forward and I began vomiting: a reaction to the seemingly physical trauma to my body. I wanted to stay frozen, right where I was; not knowing whether my father was dead or alive. I didn't know if I could handle the confirmation of the former. I would rather live with the wondering, hoping, believing. Even as I stood at the end of the block, I hoped that there was some mistake; wrong address, wrong person. But I had to keep walking, I had to get home, I had to be with my mother. My poor mother, I had to be there for her. I wiped my mouth with my t-shirt, and willed strength back into my legs. I had to get to my house, which was now just a blue blur with a brown splotch sitting in front of it.

I crawled up the steps of our house; only the screen door was closed. I burst into the house, and screamed out, "Daddy."

My brother, who was sitting on the floor, looked

up at me startled. "What's wrong with you? Daddy's not here."

"Where is the Provost Marshal?" I asked. "His car is in front of our house."

My brother got up off of the floor and walked toward me. "It's Mr. Johnson. Mommy's over there now." In a single moment I received the news that my father was all right, but his best friend was dead. A chill ran over my body, and I was overcome with conflicting emotions of relief and grief. I felt guilty for feeling relieved. A part of me was actually happy that it was their father, and not ours. With one deep breath, that initial reaction faded and I thought about Mrs. Johnson, and Sharon and Eddie, and tears of grief fell from my eyes.

Just over a month after Mr. Johnson was killed my father returned home from Vietnam. Physically, he was intact. He had been hit twice by the enemy fire, neither wound was life threatening. But emotionally he was broken; he seemed unable to cope with the loss of his best friend. He became overwhelmed with guilt. He questioned why he had made it out of Vietnam alive when thousands of other men had not. He fell into a deep depression, grappling with thoughts that challenged his worthiness to live. My father was angry and withdrawn. He was reticent about the war, telling us nothing about his experiences in Vietnam.

He returned from war a different man than when he left, but none of this mattered to us. We were just happy to have our father home.

For my mother it was different. Her husband returned home, but she lost her friend, her companion, her confidante. The man that she fell in love with did not return from Vietnam, but she hoped that he would soon, and so she waited. For over a year my mother endured the angry outbursts, the week long disappearing acts, and even the suicide attempt. Through it all, she faithfully waited, until the waiting became too dangerous for her and too dangerous for her children.

Late one night my mother was awakened by my father, who had climbed on top of her and was straddling her body. His left hand was on her neck. In his right hand he held a gun that was pointed at the center of her forehead. He was screaming at her, cussing at her, telling her he was going to kill her. She pleaded with him to stop, but when she looked into his eyes all she saw was emptiness, and she knew he was not there. "Gregory," she screamed "It's Eva, baby it's Eva. Please don't kill me Greg. Please don't kill me. I love you." She then felt a drop of liquid fall from my father's face on to her cheek. It could have been sweat, it could have been tears, but it could have been blood. Not knowing if he had already harmed himself, or worse, the children, my mother began calling out to God for help. She frantically screamed my father's name hoping her voice would reach that distant place that held him captive. "Gregory," my mother screamed as loud as she could.

Hearing his name, my brother jumped out of bed and ran to my parents room, and threw open the door. Through the blackness he saw the outline of my father's body hovering over my mother. "Daddy," Greg screamed. My brother's voice penetrated the beast that had taken over my father's body. The desperate cry of his child snapped my father back to reality. He squinted at my mother, and then looked around the room with confusion.

Seeing recognition in my father's eyes, my mother calmly said his name, "Greg, Gregory, it's me, Eva."

My father noticed the gun in his hand and broke down crying. He set the gun down on the nightstand then lifted himself from on top of my mother and laid beside her on the bed, no longer able to mask his emotions, the thoughts, the memories that haunted him. . . memories of Vietnam. This was the story my mother told Mr. Robinson, the third of the trio of friends who went to Vietnam together, when he came to remove my father from his own home.

We did not see or hear from my father for over a month. Eventually my mother tracked him down and informed him that she was taking us back to Chicago, something they had talked about doing once he retired. The day before we left, we received a call from our father. He asked to speak to each one of us, he told us that he loved us; he told us he would see us soon, and we left California without seeing our father.

In Chicago, we stayed with my grandfather in the house that my mother lived in with her family just before her mother died. Her cousin told her she should apply for welfare and get housing in one of the many projects that had popped up all over the city. Reflecting back on the difficulty she experienced in trying to get money from the government when my father was in Vietnam, along with rumors of the midnight raids— measures taken to ensure there was not a man present in the home, measures taken to guard against abuses in a system constructed for women and their children— my mother opted instead to move back home with her father. Secretly she hoped that my father would follow us to Chicago, and that we could be a family again. She did not want anything to stand in their way, including the government. So we moved into my grandfather's two-bedroom home on the Southside of Chicago.

My grandfather worked at O'Hare Airport as a maintenance man. Every other day or so, while my grandfather was at work, my mother would lock herself in the bathroom, and cry. This was her daily ritual when my father was away in Vietnam, and now, although he was only across the country, and not across the world, my mother missed him just the same, and longed to be with him just as much. My brothers and I would sit right outside the door until she came out. Although her eyes were red and puffy, she would act as if nothing was wrong, and we would act as if nothing was wrong, but we all felt the emptiness of life without my father.

We saw my father just once in the year that followed. He came to Chicago, and stayed with his brother and family out in Kankakee, just south of the city. My parents spent a lot of time alone during his visit, but he returned to California and we did not see him again for another several months.

We found out later that my parents had been in constant contact throughout these months, and when my father retired from the military in 1972, he moved back to Chicago, and started working at the same plant his brother worked at in Kankakee.

One Saturday, my parents took us all out to Washington Park for a picnic. We played for much of the afternoon, ate the chicken that my mother had fried for us that morning, my brothers played football with my father, and then my father called us all over to the blanket that we had set up under a tree. He squatted on the end of the blanket opposite where we sat, and began to talk to us. He said, "There is something I need to say to all of you. I left a part of myself over there in Vietnam, and I have struggled everyday to get back enough of myself so that I can function here with you, and be the father and husband that I once was. I'm still working through this, but I love your mother." Then he paused and choking back tears, he looked into my mother's eyes and repeated, "I love you." His words said "I love you," but his eyes said so much more. His eyes revealed deep remorse and regret for all that he had put her through; they revealed an impassioned plea for forgiveness, and they revealed an undying love that began right here in the same park some sixteen years earlier.

A couple of months after that day in the park our family moved into an apartment together, and within a year my parents had bought a house in the south suburbs of Chicago. Our family was together again, and although my parents still had their bad times, the good times outnumbered the bad, and my mother never considered life without my father again.

DIVORCE

5

DIVORCE

*My mother sang to me every
night before I fell off to sleep.*

O nce my little brother Philip was born, she
sang to both of us. My mother made a promise to herself that she would bathe us, read
to us, sing to us, and spend time with us each night
before we went to bed. When we finished our prayers
she would lay with us, and sing us to sleep. Every night
before she turned off my lamp light and carried my
brother into his room, she would say aloud, "Terry
and Philip, I love you."

She made the commitment to spend this time
with us in an effort to combat the guilt that accompa-

nied being a working mother with an executive position in a Fortune 500 company, with a fifty hour work week, and business travel that took her away from her family for a week out of each month. Her time with us was limited, and so she tried to make the best of that time, and we loved every moment she spent with us. Our father also traveled with his job, and so they set up a system to ensure that at least one of them would be home with us if at all possible.

Since my parents first started dating, they both knew that the other was a high achiever, and through the years they shuffled us, their jobs and each other around hoping to find the perfect balance between children, spouse and profession.

My parents met in 1977 when they were students at the University of Illinois. It was the beginning of my mother's sophomore year in college. My father was a junior, representing his fraternity on a panel discussing affirmative action and reverse discrimination ahead of the Supreme Court, who would hear arguments on the same subject the following week.

As my mother tried to follow the discussion, she became fixated on the only black student on the panel. After each person spoke, she hoped that he would speak next. From the first time he spoke, she never took her eyes off of him. She watched him raise his hand and cover his mouth as he cleared his throat, reach for a pitcher filled with ice water, then pour the water into his glass. She watched him as he glanced over the room. She followed his eyes looking to see if he might smile, wink, or otherwise acknowledge some-one in the audience. Maybe he would pause a little too long on a pretty girl in the audience. Maybe his girlfriend was sitting out there, proudly listening to her boyfriend present his arguments. But there was nothing, no pause, no acknowledgement, and as he surveyed the audience, his eyes met my mother's eyes. Then it happened, he paused.

When the panel discussion was over, many of the black students stood around the auditorium talking about the actual court case and what, if any, effect it would have on black enrollment on the University of Illinois' campus, and on college campuses throughout the country. There was a group of about six students debating these issues when the handsome speaker walked toward the group. One of the male students loudly con-gratulated him on a job well done. My father graciously thanked his friend, then looked directly at my mother and introduced himself.

"Michael Mitchell," my mother said his name for what seemed like the one hundredth time to her friends who had also met him earlier that evening. She had probably repeated his name one thousand times before she saw him again three weeks after their first meeting.

My mother was walking out of the campus bookstore, when he was walking in. When he saw her he was taken by surprise, and blurted out "Hey, I've been looking for you!"

She excitedly responded, "You have?" Both realizing they had exposed themselves, they laughed, embarrassed by their obvious, but mutual enthusiasm.

"Dorothy right?" my father asked.

My mother nodded and with confidence she chimed back "Michael Mitchell." A name she had become very familiar with in the three weeks since they had met.

After my parents graduated, they both moved back to the Chicagoland area and put their college degrees to work. My father became an accountant, and my mother, who came out a year after my father, was selected for a management development program in her company.

My parents married two years after my mother graduated from college, and two years later I was born. This was the year leading up to the presidential election of 1984. Both of my parents had served on the Student Government Association during college, and they were eager to be a part of an once-in-a-lifetime experience. A black man was making a serious run for President of the United States. They wanted to be a part of this movement that was changing lives of black Americans everywhere, even if it was only in their minds.

Many people, both black and white, felt that Jesse Jackson could not win, but that didn't matter. His candidacy alone changed the way blacks in America felt about themselves. Twenty years after the Civil Rights Act, blacks were given the opportunity to dream of an America led by a black man. My brother, Philip, was born between Jesse Jackson's two unsuccessful bids for the Democratic Party's nomination, and even though Jesse Jackson lost the nomination, his contribution could not be tallied up in the three million plus votes he received in the first election, or the seven million some votes he received in the second election. His true contribution could not be measured or documented. But his contribution lived in the hearts of people like my parents, who upon the birth of their son could dream about him becoming the President of the United States one day.

Even if my brother did not make it to the Oval Office, my parents had every expectation that both my brother and I would be successful, no matter what we did. They tried to guarantee this through the neighborhood we lived in, the school we went to, and the tutoring they signed us up for, even when we did not need the help. All of this was done in an effort to ensure our success. My parents believed in the philosophy that the child should exceed the parents' accomplishments, successes, living standards, wealth, and they realized that they had set the bar high, so it was their responsibility to give us the tools we needed to excel.

Both of my parents were affirmative action blacks. After the creation of affirmative action policies in the 1960s, every black that held a position of power or prestige in America's mainstream industries, corporations, government institutions, universities and organizations could be considered an affirmative action black. For black people who obtained a certain level of accomplishment, there would be someone who worked with them, had contact with them, or just knew of them, who believed that they had obtained their level of accomplishment not based on merit, but due to an affirmative action policy that pressured corporations and institutions to hire and promote incompetent or otherwise unqualified people.

My parents held different opinions about affirmative action. My mother welcomed the opportunity that affirmative action policies gave her to prove the skeptics wrong. My father, whose experiences had been more varied than my mother's, took a different position. He believed that affirmative action was a failed plan that only created resentment toward black workers, and doubt about their abilities among white workers.

My parents' opinions were based on their differing experiences in the workforce. My mother was put on the fast track at her company, receiving five promotions in ten years, and tripling her salary within that time. My father also began on the fast track, but after five years with his company, my father's "head hit the ceiling," as I had heard him say, and his career seemed to stagnate. My mother's cheerful announcements about a generous bonus, or a glowing performance review, or another promotion became commonplace in our home.

For my father, the celebrations were much less frequent. One night at the dinner table my father updated my mother on a conversation that he had had with his supervisor about moving into management. He could hardly contain his excitement as he told my mother about the position that he would be moving into as preparation for his move into management. My mother was just as excited as my father and they discussed all of the possibilities and opportunities that the move and subsequent promotion would afford my father. Eighteen months into the new job, my father still had not received the promotion into management, and after being promised one of the first promotions in the next year, his manager moved to another area and took with him my father's promise of promotion.

It was around this time that my father began coming home later and later, and spending less and less time with us. Even when he was home he seemed preoccupied. He stopped eating dinner at the table with us, and instead took his plate and ate in front of the T.V. He was also absent from weekend outings which used to be all day family affairs. He always came into our rooms and kissed us when he got home, no matter how late. I would try to wait up for him, but by the time he came home I was usually fast asleep, and never felt his lips touch my cheek. But there were times when I stayed up long enough to hear him come in. Usually I would hear him moving around in the kitchen, warming up his food, turning on the T.V. But there were other times that I heard conversations, arguments, fights between my parents that I should have never heard, and that I wished I hadn't.

My mother also noticed changes in my father. He stayed at work late, and left for work early. When he was at home, his involvement was limited and his interest even more limited. When he traveled, he began driving himself to and from the airport, a departure from our regular routine of parking the car and going to the gate or baggage claim to meet our parents after their trips.

Around my seventh birthday, my father scheduled a business trip from Monday until Friday night. He told my mother that he would leave after work and drive himself to the airport. That afternoon my mother picked us up early from our after school program, and drove us to my father's job. Instead of pulling into the company's parking lot, we parked down the block from his building. After about a half an hour, we saw my father's car pull out of the complex, and my mother followed him. My father made several stops before parking his car in an apartment parking lot, and heading into a building with a bag of take out in one hand and flowers in the other.

We sat in the parking lot, waiting for my father to come out. After what seemed like several hours, I fell asleep. When I awoke, it was light out, it was morning, and we were driving away from the airport. Seeing planes take off and land, I asked my mother if we had dropped Daddy off at the airport. She said, "Yes." Then remembering the night before, I began to ask a second question. But before I could ask my mother snapped at me, "Not now Terry." I wanted to ask why we weren't at school, but my mother's reaction to the first question discouraged me from any additional probing.

What my brother and I did not know was that after we fell asleep my mother stayed out in that parking lot all night until light replaced the dark. She saw my father leave the apartment with his arm around a woman. They drove to the airport and the woman got out of the car and sent him off with a passionate kiss on the lips.

My father arrived in town late Thursday night and home late Friday night. My mother now knew the routine. Over the week she spoke to him on the phone without mention of what she had seen. When he came home my mother was waiting to confront him. She was in bed trying to catch up on work she had fallen behind on in the last two days while she had been off work trying to cope with what she had seen.

She knew there was no use in talking to her mother. In the past, when she had complaints about my father, her mother would tell her to be patient. She was being too hard on him. She needed to understand a man's nature. She needed to stop trying to control everything. She needed to trust him. She needed to do something special for him. She needed to listen to him. She needed to be there for him. She needed to believe in him. She needed to give him another chance. She needed to love him, unconditionally.

She did love him, and even having seen him with another woman, she was not ready to let him go.

When he walked into the bedroom she looked up from her work and asked her husband, "Why?"

Unsure of what she meant my father answered with a question, "Why what?"

Losing her temper my mother threw her pen at my father, and crying screamed at him, "Why Michael?"

As if blaming my mother for even having to look

outside his marriage, he responded with comparable anger. "Why did I go and find me a *woman*? Because I feel like I'm in a marriage with another man. And I don't even know whose dick is bigger yours or mine."

Taken aback by my father's counterattack, she grimaced, "What? What are you talking about?"

My father answered, "I'm talking about the daily fight I have to be the man in this house. I'm sick of feeling like you're challenging me in everything I do, every decision I want to make for this family. I'm sick of you making more money than me. I'm sick of feeling like I'm somehow inadequate, or not making a contribution to this family. I go to work, and I can't get compensated for the job I do, forget any acknowledgment for how hard I work around there. And I know you have no idea what I am talking about because what the black man goes through in these corporations is completely different than what the black woman goes through. Especially you attractive black women. Oh, they love having you stand up there with them, as their 'support' of course."

My mother made a face at my father, protesting the insinuation he had made.

Without allowing her to speak he attacked her. "Don't look at me like that Dorothy, like I'm just making excuses. I come from the same philosophy that you do, and I have worked hard, ten times as hard as most of those people in that office. But you know what I've learned? None of that matters if you don't have someone in your corner pulling for you, someone willing to take a stand for you. And you better hope the person supporting you has some power, because if he doesn't then he might find himself in the same boat as you. Being promised promotions that never materialize, being offered lateral moves, with no additional room for growth, and no additional compensation, sitting through performance reviews with managers that show no interest in your career. That's what I deal with everyday. And when I come home I want to put that all behind me, and at least be the king of this castle. But I can't because my wife, 'a high level corporate exec,' doesn't know how to leave her business persona at the job, and walk into this house and be my wife. I need that tenderness, and support. I need my wife to believe in me and to take care of me—honor me, put me first. I need to feel like I am your world, not all of the time, but some of the time. That's what I need, that's what I went looking for, and that's what Monica gives me right now."

As my father spoke, my mother began to feel badly. She had failed him, not been there for him the way he needed. She understood, she wanted to make it better, but hearing the woman's name hit her like a ton of bricks, and she ran to the bathroom crying, and locked the door.

I heard everything, including the door slam, and without thinking I went to be with my mother, but we were not allowed to go into my parents' room if the door was shut, and so I pressed my back against the wall next to the door, and slid down into a sitting position on the floor. I sat in front of my parents' closed door and waited. Within a couple of minutes my father opened the door, seeing me sitting there he bent down slightly and kissed me on the top of my head. He went into the kitchen for a couple of minutes and then I heard the garage door open, he got in his car and drove away.

After hearing my father's car speed off, my mother came out of the bathroom, and crawled back into bed. I walked toward my parents' bed and whispered, "Mommy, are you O.K.?"

With sadness in her voice, for what she was experiencing, and now for her daughter being exposed to it, she answered with a weak, "Yes, baby, go back to sleep." I took advantage of my mother not specifying where I should go to sleep and I crawled in bed next to her. She wrapped her arms around me, comforting her and me. I wished I could make her feel better, I wished my father still loved her.

My father continued to come home late and leave early for several weeks. Then one night he arrived home while my mother was putting us to bed. He stood outside my bedroom door, just out of sight and listened to us say our prayers. Then my mother sang the same song that she sang to us every night. "Yesterday a child came out to wonder, caught a dragonfly inside a jar, fearful when the sky was full of thunder, and tearful at the falling of a star. And the seasons they go round and round, and the painted ponies go up and down, we're captive on a carousel of time, we can't return we can only look, behind from where we came, and go round and round and round in the circle game."

My father realized that he had never paid much attention to our nightly ritual. He had never noticed my four-year old brother's flawless recitation of the Lord's Prayer, never listened to the song my mother sang. But now as he listened to the words of a song about time and change, he thought about the first time he saw my mother's face in the half filled auditorium on the University of Illinois' campus. He thought about how much he loved her on their wedding day. He thought about his vows, his promises to her. And he thought about my brother and me and how fast we were growing up, without him.

With my brother fast asleep, and me quickly falling, my mother turned off the lamp light and lifted my brother to carry him into his room. My father met her in the hallway. He took my brother out of my mother's arms, took hold of her hand and together they laid my brother in his bed. Still holding hands they went to their bedroom, and after that night our life seemed back to normal. There was one change; my father became a part of our nightly ritual. After we bathed, he would come in my room with us and my parents would take turns reading as we turned the pages of our favorite books. My father would say our prayers with us. And we would all listen as my mother sang her favorite song. We went on like this for years. Sometimes my father would have relapses, and begin leaving early and coming home late. At times, he would disappear all weekend. There would be periods where he traveled a lot. But when he was home with us he gave us his undivided attention, and our family seemed whole again.

In 1993, when I was ten years old, my mother's doctor found a lump in her breast. For years, my mother had masked her unhappiness. By focusing all of her attention on her job and my brother and me, she ignored my father's late nights with no explanation. She made excuses for his absence at parent teacher conferences or school programs. She rationalized the absence of sexual intimacy in their marriage. But with this bad news, my mother could no longer hold it together and she broke down in her doctor's office. The doctor tried to comfort her, explaining that they first needed to do a sonogram, then if necessary a mammogram, then if necessary a biopsy, then if necessary remove the tumor. He never mentioned what the process would be if the tumor was malignant and not benign. He assured her that that conversation would be premature.

The first person my mother called when she left the office was her brother Greg, who was an oncologist. My Uncle Greg returned her call while she was cooking dinner, and we were completing homework at the kitchen table. With my brother and me close by, my mother discreetly repeated the story to my uncle to whom she looked for a mixture of comfort and information. My Uncle Greg assured her that the doctor was right, but that she could come to his office the following day. By the time my father arrived home that night we had all gone to bed, and my mother never mentioned her visit to the doctor.

My mother opted to have the tumor removed completely before they performed a biopsy. On the morning that my mother would go into surgery, she informed my father about the tumor and the surgery. My father just stared at her, first shocked by what she had said, but that shock was quickly overshadowed by the sheer resentment he had toward the woman standing in front of him. He resented her for not telling him about the tumor, but more, he resented her for not needing him even during this time.

Several days passed before my mother received

the news that the tumor was benign. She spent those days doing deep soul searching about the purpose of her life, and about what she owed her children. Through the years she weighed the positives and negatives of her marriage, making tradeoffs and compromising herself for the good of her family. But now she made a promise to God that she would not devalue herself for one minute longer. She would not waste this life that God had given her. She bargained with God that if He let her live just until the children grew up, she would make more of her life, she would use all of the talents and skills that He had blessed her with, and she would appreciate every breath she took.

After the call from the doctor, she knew she had to keep her promise to herself and to God. That night my father walked into a dark house. As soon as he opened the door he could smell the sweet smoky scent of a clove cigarette. He called out my mother's name and reached for the light switch, which he usually did not turn on during his late night entrances. Softly my mother answered, "I'm right here," and turned on the lamp on the table next to her. She took a long drag off of the dark brown cigarette, a habit she picked up in college, and had not indulged in since, then looking away from her husband she blew the smoke out slowly. She turned to her husband, and with tears in her eyes she told him, "I can't do this anymore Michael."

Without responding, my father came around the couch and sat down across from my mother. "I've tried Michael. I've tried to give you time. I've tried to give you your space. I've tried to give you what you needed, what you wanted, because I love you. But at some point I have to love me. In these last couple of days I realize more than ever that this is the only life I've got. This is it! And I know that God wants more for me and I want more for myself."

My father stared at my mother deeply. He wished he could say something to comfort her, but he knew the truth, no matter how hard he tried to ignore his heart, he knew that he had fallen out of love with his wife. And so he nodded his head in agreement. His only verbal response to my mother was "I know," and the next day they began the process of dissolving their twelve year marriage.

After the 1970s and the women's liberation movement, it became easier and easier to end marriages as women became more and more self-sufficient. The man no longer worried about whether his family would be impoverished in his absence. The pressure and responsibility to stay was hugely diminished and the man could leave his wife with a clear conscience, knowing that financially, his family would be fine.

For the woman, situations that she had no choice but to endure in the 1950s and earlier became intolerable. Women, who in the past had no choice but to stay with unfaithful or abusive husbands, were now opting to go out on their own. Women were becoming competitive in the workforce and making enough money to support themselves and their families. This influenced my mother's decision, just as it did many women. My mother worried about many aspects of being a single mother, but financial security was not one of them.

My brother was nine and I was eleven when our parents divorced; and so we were old enough to resent our parents, but not old enough to understand them; old enough to feel they failed us, but not old enough to realize that it was bigger than us; old enough to protest about having to go stay at Dad's for the weekend, but not old enough to realize how fortunate we were to have a father who wanted to spend time with us and demanded that we spend time with him. We were old enough to feel broken hearted over the failure of our parent's marriage, but not old enough to realize that there would be a part of us that would always mourn the loss of our "family". Secretly, I hoped that my parents would get back together, right up to the day, over six years after my parents divorced, that my father married my stepmother, Paula.

Just a year after my father remarried, I headed down to North Carolina to attend school at Duke University. I left for Duke full of anticipation for the new experience, and full of anxiety from leaving my mother, who like my father dated throughout the years, but unlike my father had not yet met the person she wanted to spend the rest of the rest of her life with.

On the day that my mother and brother would leave me in North Carolina, we ate an early breakfast in the hotel. I began crying half way through breakfast and didn't stop until my mother and Philip were probably an hour up the road. Knowing me, and knowing that my tears were a combination of me needing my mom, and me feeling that she needed me, my mother assured me that she would be fine. She told me, "Children are supposed to grow up, that's what they do. That's what parents want. Everything I have done was so we could be right here where we are today, with you starting college, making me proud, experiencing life. That's what my work was for. Just do your best, and enjoy yourself, and I will be fine!" I would do my best, for my mother and for myself. Ever since my parents divorced I worked hard to please my mother, and make her proud. Duke was just one more opportunity to do both.

I met Keith Strickland during the first week of classes. He was one of a handful of African American students enrolled in the same Principles of Biology course. Our first date was a study date and I think I fell in love with him right there in Perkins Library. Keith was ambitious, driven and confident, funny, sincere and sensitive. And the more I got to know him, the more I liked the person he was.

Keith was my first love. He was the first man I made love with, and it was everything my mother led me to believe it wasn't. It was beautiful, it was soft and sensual. Keith made love to me slowly and carefully, whispering in my ear, "I love you," tenderly kissing me all over my face and neck, stroking my hair, asking me if I felt all right, asking if I wanted to stop. I shook my head side to side. I didn't want him to stop. I never felt so close to anyone in my life, it was as if we were one person, and I did not want it to end.

As he moved inside of me, my body began to relax. Then our bodies began to move together. Our lovemaking created its own rhythm, its own beat, and suddenly Prince's *Adore* seemed far off in the distance somewhere, ultimately drowned out by Keith's breathing as it grew heavier and heavier. My head began to swirl, and my entire body became sensitive to his touch. He moved deeper and faster inside of me until I lost control of my body, and he lost control of his, and we held on to each other as our bodies trembled, then we held on to each other until our bodies became still again. Keith began to gently rock me and tell me how much he loved me and I told him the same. I did love him, more than I ever knew I could love someone. I gave myself to him that night . . . I gave myself to him forever.

Keith and I dated throughout college, and

when we began the process of applying to medical schools, we submitted our applications and test scores to the same schools. We were both accepted and chose to attend Emory University School of Medicine, and shortly after that he asked me to marry him. I said yes, knowing wholly and completely that I wanted to spend the rest of my life with this man. There was no hesitation. I trusted and believed in him with everything inside of me. I knew he loved me, and I could not wait to be his wife.

Sometimes I wondered if my mother ever loved my father the way I loved Keith. Was she willing to move mountains to be with him? Was she willing to forfeit some of her dreams for his? Was she willing to love him totally and completely? Years after my parents divorced, I asked my mother what happened between her and my father, and she said that she just wasn't happy anymore, and believed that she had a better chance at happiness without my father than with him. I do not know if my mother ever found happiness, but I believe at some point she found peace, and maybe that's enough.

A couple of months before the wedding, I invited my mother and grandmother out for a day with the girls. We went to several dress shops and then to lunch. As they tried on dresses, I critiqued each one, too small, too short, too bright. I watched the twosome as they took turns modeling the next fashion. They were excited. They were happy for me. As they smiled I noticed their wrinkles, some from laughing and some from worrying. I noticed their voices, both sweet, but powerful. I noticed their hands, long and lean with prominent veins stretching across them. I looked into their smiling eyes and knew that they each had a story to tell, a story that I wanted to hear.

After they were each satisfied with their choice we went to lunch. Three generations of Reynolds women sat in a restaurant booth. I admiringly looked across the table at these two women who had chosen different courses for their lives, and who both seemed content with themselves and their decision. I marveled at their ability to smile, and laugh, and love. I wanted to be like them. I wanted to know what made them who they were, and so I began asking questions. "What kind of childhood did you have mom? What was it like growing up in California? Who were your parents Grandma? What did they do? Did they have brothers and sisters? What was it like when you first moved to Chicago? How did you meet Granddaddy? What did you do for fun growing up?"

My grandmother cut me off, "Girl, you're making me dizzy, you asking all of these questions. I can't even remember half of that stuff."

My mother giggled, "I *can* remember, and still don't feel like answering all of those questions!" They both laughed, and I laughed too. Cherishing the moment, I smiled and shook my head, understanding that I would have to wait just a *little* longer for the answers to my questions.

Terry would never know the trials and triumphs of her ancestors; long ago experiences that shaped and influenced the woman she had become. Past heroism and sacrifice that allowed her the life, experiences, and opportunity that she enjoyed. Having been born into a family, into a culture, that seemed unwilling or unable to verbally pass down their history; the successes and the failures, the gains and the losses, the experiences that almost destroyed them and those that strengthened them. Instead, the experiences and the accompanying lessons die with each generation. And the next generation is left with little understanding and knowledge of their legacy.

Terry would never know that, just like her, the women who came before her had great expectations for life, love and family. She would not know how her ancestors fought to hold their families together within an environment that seemed determined to tear them apart. She could not know how her family was tested generation after generation. How loving wives lost their husbands, and their innocence. How committed husbands were stripped of their family and their manhood.

As Terry enthusiastically entered into adulthood, she was unaware of the twists and turns that life had in store for her. She could not anticipate the experiences that would test her faith in herself, her faith in her husband and even her faith in God. Terry could not know, and would not know, unless necessary, that there was a quiet strength that lived deep inside of her, passed down through the generations. It was a strength that would allow her to cope and to survive whatever life brought her way; an inner strength that she could pull from, a strength that she could depend on if ever she had to dance alone.

ABOUT THE AUTHOR

Christine LeVeaux is a professor of American Government and Black Politics. She received her Bachelor of Arts from Spelman College and her Doctorate of Philosophy from Louisiana State University. She is the author of several nonfiction articles. This is her first novel.

www.christineleveaux.com